THE
RADIO

Other Titles in the Adam Quatrology

The Electroencephalographer Couldn't Cry
Adam's Big Bang
Return of the Horla

THE
RADIO

A NOVEL

BERNARD SUSSMAN

Bartleby Press
Washington • Baltimore

Copyright © 2012, 2019 by Bernard Sussman

Cover design by Ross Feldner

ISBN 978-0935437-55-3
Library of Congress Control Number: 2011940646

Published by:

Bartleby Press

PO Box 858
Savage, Maryland 20763
800-953-9929
www.BartlebythePublisher.com

Printed in the United States of America

To Patricia Stein
& Monsignor Kevin Hart

One

On the fifth morning of the second month of his sixty-third year Adam Merritt awakened feeling different. Although it was Monday morning and already eight o'clock, he had none of his usual urges to be up and about. What struck him also was that the cracks in the ceiling were no longer getting to him. They were directly above his bed and ordinarily he'd worry they might progress to a free-fall of crumbling plaster aimed at impaling some important part of him, even his head, with serious, possibly deadly, effect.

This had already happened two years before, not more than a few moments after he'd gotten up and headed for the john. Although repaired back then, several of the cracks had reappeared, and considering his limited confidence in the fellow who'd done the job, every morning tended to start off with a mix of relief for having survived the night and foreboding about what might still be brewing directly above his head. But on this bright day the cracks, albeit no less apparent, didn't bother him at all.

His second observation was that until now, his daily morning beginnings had never managed to seem bright.

1

Whatever their luminance, they represented just another dreary summons to get on with what had to be done. But presently, all he could do was simply lay there and marvel that whoever had the privilege of possessing this place, ceiling cracks or no ceiling cracks, should have such a neat set up.

He looked at the old and weathered green paint separating from the plaster, barely glanced at cobwebs in neglected corners, and took to admiring the Kashan rug in spite of the fact that it was resolutely determined not to stay put but rather to slide about persistently and rumple up into hazardous toe-catching hurdles upon the underlaid wall to wall carpeting. All of these previously, irksome things, seemed now, however, to give his bedroom a familiar patina that imbued it, strangely enough, with a comfortably familiar, lived-in feeling.

So Adam pressed his cheek against a seductively cool and soft percale pilow, perfectly satisfied to remain right where he was, but continuing to both envy and congratulate the person who might own all of this. On other mornings that would be himself. Today, in view of the radical shift from his habitual outlook, he was unhinged enough to be unsure of his very identity.

What was going on could have nothing to do with drugs. He'd given up on all of his antidepressant medications for more than a year. He was clean. And that extra single malt he'd had with Harold the night before couldn't possibly be accountable, either, even though he didn't remember anything the two of them had talked about. Harold, ever boring anyway, was apt to affect him that way.

Might it be that his prayers were being finally answered? And that all on his own, spontaneously, he was getting better, becoming more casual, less driven and picayunish about ordinarily bothersome trivia? What prayers? What the hell was going on? What could he be thinking? Never in his life had he prayed for anything! He didn't believe in it. His wife, Annie, took care of that sort of thing. Well then, maybe hers were being answered and something really metaphysical was taking place here. But who could be answering her prayers? God? Christ? Both of them?

No answer forthcoming, just a friendly bump from Willy, his Doberman. The dog was burrowing his snoot beneath the bed covers having come upstairs to see why Adam wasn't already down below, finished with breakfast, and getting ready to leave for his office. Ordinarily, by this time of day, Willy would be the only one left to wonder about something like that. Annie would be out shopping or swimming, or in church praying for the three of them.

Right after being nosed by Willy, the phone rang.

"Doctor Merritt! You oversleep?"

It was Agnes, his office nurse.

"No, actually. I was just thinking what a beautiful day it is! Much too nice, really, to do anything but maybe just lie around here a little longer and then head out of doors for awhile. What's the temperature?"

"I've no idea. When do you plan on getting down here?"

She was not her usual all-business self, nor was she sounding one of her rare, gruff objections. It was a first. Agnes was clearly surprised and taken aback.

"Well what's the chance of me holding off maybe 'til noon?"

"Zero. There are four patients waiting already."

Merritt was a skin doctor, a dermatologist. But a

dermatologist thinking only how nice it would be to simply stay put. His percale pillow was ever more inviting. "Oh just do what I do. Pack 'em all off with samples of a good steroid cream."

"Doctor Merritt! I can't believe I'm hearing this! Without careful examination? Or a skin scraping? I couldn't be a party to something like that! But if you're not well enough to come in, I'll just reschedule everyone. Is that what you want?"

"No, no. That wouldn't be right. I'll be there as soon as I can. Just have them all wait."

The business of the steroid cream had surprised him. Hard to figure. It was so easily asserted. And to know he was no longer on Prozac. And that Harold was a dull, dull guy. Or even that Harold existed. Or an Annie. Or a Willy. And that the ceiling cracks had been such a burden. But most of all, why it was so tough to get up in the morning. How in the world had he come by the knowledge of all these things? And apparently gotten himself into such a fix! It was like waking up and finding oneself a character in a damned movie, but hopelessly miscast and far out of type for a carefree, happy-go-lucky guy like him! But he'd do what he could. Hell! What choice did he have? He felt himself being directed.

"Out of my way, dog! We gotta' get moving!"

Adam showered, dressed, made coffee, and drove to the office.

Two

"Good morning, Agnes old girl! Who's on first?"

"What do you mean?"

"It's a joke. You remember, an old Abbott and Costello routine. C'mon! Don't make like you've never heard it!"

Agnes, at around forty nine, was quite prim and had always seemed a little drawn. Her hair was beginning to gray and she'd taken to pulling it back into a tight little bun resting just above the nape of her neck. Today, Adam wondered what she was trying to hide back there as with stiffened bearing and not imperceptibly widened eyes she rather unkindly jabbed a first office chart into his hands. "Doctor, there are now six patients waiting. Do we begin, or don't we?"

Besides a small waiting room and places for the nurse and secretary, Adam's office consisted of three examining rooms and one other for treatments or minor surgical procedures. There was also his private office. Agnes had ushered a patient into each of the examination rooms. With chart in hand he stepped inside Examination Room 1.

Mrs. Lombardo was a small middle aged woman, attractive, fashionable, and blonde.

"Well now, my dear! How can I help you? By the way, that is one helluva handsome shoulder bag you're sporting!"

"Thank you, doctor. It's genuine alligator. I've got this awful itch. It comes on mostly at night and that's when these little red spots have a way of popping out almost anywhere."

Mrs. Lombardo was pointing to her left forearm but Adam was distracted. Something was jogging his memory.

"If I'm not mistaken alligator bags were outlawed some time ago. Or was it that you couldn't import them from certain places? Damned if I remember which. Anyway, you want to know something? Back in 1934 there was this Tarzan movie, *Tarzan And His Mate*, with Johnny Weissmuller and Maureen O'Sullivan. Well there's a scene in the movie where Tarzan has to wrestle with this really huge crocodile underwater, and he finally wins out by stabbing it to death. Good God! The water turned black with the poor creature's blood! It gushed out all over the place! I could hardly bear to watch. Towards the end I was even rooting for the crocodile. What do you think about that?"

Mrs. Lombardo thought with her eyes. They were popped wider than those of Agnes.

"Doctor! I itch! Aren't you going to look at my spots?"

She extended her left forearm.

"I don't see a blessed thing. Oh wait! You mean this tiny little one right here?"

"Yes. That's one of them. What is it?"

"Damned if I know!"

"Well I never!"

Adam decided to explain.

"What I mean is that just by looking at it, it's impossible to say. I'd have to snip it out, take a biopsy and send it off to the lab so it could be studied under the microscope."

"Is that what you recommend?"

"You want my honest opinion?"

"Of course! What else would I be here for?"

Adam felt empowered to continue.

"It's a waste of time. The pathologist is only gonna say it could be `this' or maybe it's `that' or even something else after he fills up a whole page describing what it looks like under high magnification. He'll see all kinds of inflammatory change or what they call acanthosis. It's the same old story every damned time. Never what it is exactly. Never even what it exactly isn't. So when the chips are finally down it's gonna' be up to me to bloody well guess at what you may be allergic to, or what could be biting you at night. It could even be one of those little bugs that seem to pop up everywhere. And that's the God's honest truth."

"So what do I do, doctor?"

"Well if I were you I'd go home and have the place fumigated right away. Then, if the thing doesn't let up you can try a good steroid cream. I can let you have a few samples."

"All right... What's next?"

"Nothing. Just give the nurse your chart. And good luck to you. Let me know how it all turns out."

"Thank you doctor. I will."

Adam moved down the hall towards an adjoining room where his next patient awaited him. After a few steps Agnes caught up with him.

"Doctor?"

"That's me!"

"Okay... All joking aside, what on earth is going on around here? I'm totally confused."

"For instance?"

"I'm not referring to your being so late or the kidding around, although it's quite unlike you. What I'm talking about is Mrs. Lombardo. She's supposed to get herself an exterminator?"

"Right. And like I said on the phone. Give her a couple of sample tubes, kenalog, whatever's handy."

"And no biopsy for the lab?"

"Right. I'm sick of taking out pieces of skin and putting in sutures. For all the years we've done it I've never learned anything that's determined how I treat a patient. So it's high time we stopped all that nonsense."

"But..."

"Don't say it! We'll do all right even without the surgical fees and so will the pathologists in the derm lab. Anyway, for what they do, their charges are outrageous."

"So you won't be doing any surgery today?"

"Scared we won't clear enough to make your salary?"

"That's ridiculous, doctor! And you know it!"

"You can't fool me, Agnes! But relax. I'll still have to biopsy anything that looks malignant. Feel better?"

"Whatever you say, doctor. Whatever you say."

Without the surgical rigmarole to occupy him, Adam got through office hours in record time. Ordinarily he'd be working right through lunch and finish up around three o'clock. Today, though, he was through at one o'clock and did it with a flourish. The last patient, a Mr. Goldberg, had an obvious poison ivy rash.

"What do I owe you, Doc?"

"Forget it. Glad to be of service. And better you came to me than some fool druggist!"

No sooner than Goldberg had gone, and the office was empty, Agnes was at him again.

"You think I didn't see that?"

"What?"

"What do you think? The freebee! That's what!"

Before this particular moment it would have been difficult to brief her. But if not entirely sure of his position, he was at least prepared to formulate a tentative plan for changing procedure in his office. The need was there.

"It wasn't charity. Goldberg can afford to pay. He's got a big real estate agency..."

"I get it. You're looking for a favor?"

"You don't get it at all. I was about to say, before you popped off, that he's got both money and insurance. I wasn't looking for any damned favors! So how does this grab you? I really enjoy being helpful and nice to people but more and more this fee for service bullshit, this quid pro quo arrangement we have, is getting in the way. Sometimes I feel like a damned barber. Now don't ask me why. I haven't a clue. But after all these years it suddenly happened. I did it for nothing, I liked it and I'm glad. Anyway, someone with my knowledge and experience ought to be ashamed to treat poison ivy and charge for it. Christ! My mother never charged me!"

"Your mother was a doctor too? I didn't know that."

Agnes was a lost cause.

"No. She was just my mother. Which was very much more than her being anything else since she was so awfully good at it."

Agnes strained for a handle on all of this.

"Well then doctor, would you please tell me which services we'll be charging for in the future and which we won't? And how often do you intend to use the operating room? I'm getting ready to order supplies."

Agnes had to be on track whereas Adam, ever since getting up that morning, had no particular focus except to make his professional circumstance as pleasant as possible for all concerned.

"Don't sweat it. We'll just see how the spirit moves us. Order like usual. What's left over, we can always donate to a good cause."

Then he headed home.

Three

"What are you doing here?"

Not a very cordial greeting from his wife.

"I finished early. What's for lunch?"

"Damn!"

"Expecting someone? Where's Willy?"

"In the yard. He interferes when I vacuum. Now look here, are you going to be in the way, also?"

Say what she might, she was glad to see him. They were always glad to see one another. Adam could read it in her blue Irish eyes howsoever she contorted what an aunt of hers had called a wholesome, straightforward, face.

"How's that song go? I'll never be in your way?"

"Very smart. Well you will be if I don't finish my work around here."

"Look. All I want is some tomato soup, an English muffin, and a cup of tea. Is that too much to ask?"

They had been standing in the front hall beside an upturned rug, duster, and her readied for action Hoover.

"Okay. Come on out to the kitchen. It'll take just a minute. Don't trip over that cord."

While the soup was being microwaved and the kettle put to boil Adam settled into his usual place at the kitchen table. They'd furnished a pleasant little dining alcove with colonial style furniture overhung by a wall mounted wine rack. After staring up at it for a short while he called out to her. She was at the sink pouring hot water over a tea bag.

"Hey! You know these wine bottles are getting real dusty?"

Now with tea and soup before him he found her hovering closeby, but with hands to hip.

"You some kinda cripple? If they bother you, dust them."

"Well don't get testy about it. They don't bother me at all. I was just making a simple observation and letting you in on it. That's all."

"How come they don't bother you? You turn some kind of a new leaf? Usually, everything bothers you. And if it doesn't, why are you all of a sudden confiding in me that like everything else around here, and most other places too, bottles and other dumb things do manage to get dusty once in awhile? What are you up to, Adam?"

"I'm not up to anything. Just speaking my mind. That's all. It's good, real good, to give free vent to it every so often. Maybe even all the time. Like right now I'm thinking those jeans you've got on are too tight for you but they sure give you a sexy rear end. Would you like to hit the sack and fool around a little?"

"No I wouldn't. I'm going to finish my vacuuming. Do you think you might be able to reach over to the toaster by yourself and get the muffin when it pops?"

"Come on!"

"What in heaven's name has gotten into you, Adam?"

"I'm not the answer to all your prayers?"

"Adam, I don't pray to have you. For better or worse, I've got you. Now, why are you really home so early? Just tell me that and I'll get back to my vacuum!"

"I've already told you. I finished up early. That's all. Even did it after starting late. And from now on I'm thinking to work no more than half a day. Streamline my whole operation. Neat, hey?"

"And you're gonna park here for the rest of the day? Be under my feet, you and that dog? Both of you?"

"I dunno about him but where else should I be?"

Annie thought it over

"What's Harold doing?"

"I don't care. Whatever it is it'll have to be without me."

"Okay. Then after you finish your tea, go on out and sit with Willy. You can let him in on every blessed thing that's on your mind. Maybe he can make some sense out of it. I give up. See you later."

Annie headed back towards the front of the house. In a few moments he could hear the alternating drone of the Hoover.

He glanced at the wine bottles once more. Actually, they were all quite empty having been previously consumed and were there now just for decorative purposes. His unopened bottles were stored away in a dining room closet. But fixing on one of these drained specimens he found himself staring at an especially dusty Lafite Rothschild 1959. What a year! What a wine! They'd polished this one off way back in 1961, up in the Rainbow Grill to the strains of Jonah Jones and his marvelous quartet. The good old days? Not really. And not when he remembered his delightful morning pressed against that cool percale pillow.

God, so much dust in his house! Hard to figure where it all came from. They never opened windows. They were sealed up tight as a tomb and had air conditioning. It was a real mystery. But not as big as why the matter of unrelenting wear and tear, or dust, including that which covered the wine bottles, seemed not to bother him any longer.

But why had it been so annoying in the first place? Freud would probably have had an answer. The guy who'd put him on the Prozac sure didn't.

Well if Annie was going to spend her afternoon tidying up the downstairs, and he was to stay out of her way, there was no choice but to head back to the bedroom. Having finished most of what he wanted to eat, he took his tea along with him.

Soon changed into jeans and slippers he picked up a book by Henry Roth, got himself seated in a comfortable chair near a window, and tea in hand began to read.

Ten minutes later the phone rang. Harold.

"Hey dad! Whatcha' doin? Called your office and you were gone. You sick or somethin'?"

Adam had never been a "dad". Neither had Harold. Why he always began conversations like this could be still another mystery.

"No. I'm just working more efficiently. Gives me time to read, et cetera."

"Whatcha readin'? Dermatology stuff?"

Harold was a retired chest surgeon.

"No. It's a book by Henry Roth. I'm reading where he admits to having a relationship with his sister."

"What kind?"

"What kind do you think? Incestuous, you idiot!"

"Jesus Christ! I'd rather not hear about it! So what's he got to say?"

"Make up your mind."

"Is it something I oughta know?"

"No."

"Okay. Clue me in."

"They were at it for years. On weekend mornings when nobody was home. In a tenement on the upper East Side. In fact, they were doing one another no more than a block or two from where you grew up. Chances are you were passing by, or playing stick ball out front, just about the time they were hot and heavy."

"Goddamn! How old were they?" Harold was hooked.

"She was fourteen. Roth was a little older."

"Why would he write something like that now? He must be more than eighty."

"Wrong. He's dead. Maybe near the end he just needed to get it off his chest. You know, like when you go to church."

"Yeah," Harold said. "But it doesn't count unless you do it with a priest."

"How do you know that? Besides, by now his writings have probably been chewed over by hundreds of priests as well as horny old guys like you and me."

Harold was sixty-seven. "How could anybody do something like that? They'd have to be sick!"

"Dogs do it. Cats do it. Birds and bees do it. You don't know the song?"

"Yeah? Well animals don't have a soul and a conscience to go along with it that tells them right from wrong."

"Harold, you go to confession regularly?"

"I try to."

"Generally have one or two hot items to talk about?"

"I suppose."

"So one real difference between you and other animals is that you're ashamed of yourself and can spill it. Right?"

"Where you goin' with all this stuff, Adam?"

"Harold, I'm not going anywhere. All I've done is give you free and uncensored access to my mind. I'm beginning to get the idea that nobody has much taste for that sort of thing."

"But it's something you've decided to be into?"

"Okay... Let's start over. What the hell did you call me for in the first place?"

"I was just wondering how you might be feeling after all that scotch last night. Have a big head this morning?"

"Not at all. And I only had one extra."

"You kiddin'? You practically knocked off the whole bottle! And then you conked out. It took three cups of Medaglia D'Oro to bring you around. You don't remember?"

"What'd we talk about?"

"We? I couldn't get a word in. You were like in a groove. Said you weren't gonna' take it anymore. Whatever that meant. And just before you passed out you were claiming to be some kinda weird thing, like a medium, and if I listened up I'd get to hear things I needed to know. You had an inside track. But next thing I knew you were snorin' away."

"If it's true, it's fascinating."

"What do you mean `if'?"

"That's right. You never lie. Correct?"

Harold was put off. Generally they'd talk about cars or boats. Never anything like this, nor question one another's integrity. Put off or not, Harold just had to know more.

"Correct! I don't! But there was another thing. I don't know whether I should mention it, but I guess I'd better. Actually, before you dozed off, you were crying like a baby. And besides the really weird stuff, you were mumbling about wanting, just once, to get up in the morning and have a straight take on things, see it all crystal clear. Somethin' about uncensored natural goodness. Whatever the hell that might be."

"And that's it?"

"Well the last thing you said was, `If it's dust to dust anyway, what's so bad about a little dust'? Then you were out like a light. And I beat it for the coffee. Once I had you sitting up and drinking some, you came around pretty fast. So in about half an hour you were ready for bed and I ducked home."

"And Annie never came downstairs?"

"Not that I saw."

"Well okay!"

"Okay? You call all this Okay? I'd say you better start seein' someone and pronto!"

"Listen up. I'm doing better that that. Better than seein' someone I'm seein' just about everything a helluva lot better."

"You wanta let me in on it, dad?"

"Forget the fucking `dad' business! Just for once, forget it!"

"Okay, okay."

Adam sort of whispered into his mouthpiece.

"It looks like I got my wish. I've been seeing the natural light of day. It's gorgeous!"

"You kiddin' me? So does everyone else. That's if they've got their eyes open, they do."

"The hell they do. I think it's only me."

"Dammit it Adam! You've lost your mind. Should I come on over?"

"Hell no. You stay right where you are. And don't start blabbing about this or praying for me! I couldn't take it. And remember, no interference."

"Annie know what's going on?"

"No. Hey! I said to stay out of it! Besides which, she's got to do her vacuuming. Bye Harold. See you later."

"Listen Adam. There's this real high intensity light bulb I read about. All you have to do is shine it on yourself if when you get up in the morning you're down in the dumps. Should I see if I can dig out the article? It has something to do with seasonal depression."

"It's not necessary. We're doing all right on our own. Fun in the sun won't cut it. Take care. Gotta go."

Adam hung up.

Poor Harold. How explain to a guy for whom miracles came catalogued and by the book that just the right amount of scotch and three cups of Medaglia D'Oro, under certain specific conditions, may jog a brain miraculously well?

Four

Adam considered pressing on with Roth's *Mercy of a Rude Stream*. But if the truth were to be known, and that was exactly what he'd been toying with, he'd have to agree with Harold. He was beginning to find this last work of Henry Roth a little too sordidly sensational and not quite what he'd like to discuss with anyone. In fact, his only reason for talking to Harold about it was just to rile him a little. But why? Harold was a reliable friend and he did happen to like him, even though he could be a little too straight-laced at times.

Adam felt a twinge. Here was steady old Harold, trying to do the right thing, checking on him to see if he was all right, and what did he do? He'd rebuffed him. Worse than that, he'd kind of ridiculed him. Not only in so many words, but immediately afterward, in his own thoughts, as he reflected upon their conversation. There seemed to come a point, in this inclination to be candid, where one had to choose between outspoken honesty and either tight-lipped reticence or a voiced insincerity. And then one tended to waffle, based on a concern not only for the next guy's feelings, but for one's own as well.

Sometime, past the beginning, came guilt. And it was not a pleasant thing. It hurt badly enough to tongue-tie some and make liars of almost all the rest. So who was he, now, all of a sudden, to be different? What were his special exemptions from all of that? From where might come his daring to push the envelope on being blunt? The day which had started off so remarkably was sporting a downside. Adam went back to reading his book.

A little later, Annie materialized in the doorway of their bedroom. From her expression he sensed that something was brewing.

"Don't tell me you're going to vacuum me out of here!"

"Nope. It's just time for my afternoon nap."

"Since when?"

"Since I've been doing it for years. You were blissfully unaware of it because up `til today you were a proper working man. Now you're probably going to discover all my other secrets as well."

"Like what? I'm fascinated."

"Don't be. My life is an open book and you know it. Just get out of here and let me rest! Play with Willy or do something constructive. And remember. Tonight we're supposed to go to Susan's for dinner."

"Damn! Tonight? So soon? We were just there! Weren't we?"

"Au contraire. It was like six months ago. Tell me. What about those two annoys you so? They're a decent enough pair and after all, he is your stockbroker."

"Sure. But that's over the phone. I don't have to look at him. Over a meal, I just can't take it. I lose my appetite!"

"I don't know what you're talking about. Ed's far from being good looking but he makes a decent enough appearance."

"Yeah? Well how about those long hairs hangin' down from his nose? They're not enough to make you sick?"

"You know? I never even noticed."

"Well tonight, take a look. And I bet you're gonna get sick to your stomach, also."

"Thanks a lot!"

"Hey! Maybe I'll just take him aside before drinks and make a little suggestion that he go upstairs and tidy up a bit. I could sorta suggest he needs a closer shave and while he's at it he could trim those goddammed hairs of his! You wanna know something? Every so often I think of making him an anonymous gift of one of those little battery operated nasal hair clippers. That might work. No? What do you think?"

"Are you quite through? Can I take my nap now?"

"I'm just speaking my mind. That's all."

"Adam, is this something I'll have to put up with from now on? You're going to run every passing thought by me?"

"What's wrong with that? Don't you think it would be a good idea, before we're dead and gone? To really get to know one another?"

"After thirty years we're going to tighten up this relationship of ours? And get seriously acquainted? Not on your life! Let's just settle for what we have, a pleasant enough standoff. We don't need some kind of a letdown, or even worse, real conflict."

"How could that happen?"

"Easy. Believe me, easy! And especially, right now,

Five

"Remember, Adam. Behave yourself."

They had parked their car in Ed and Susan's driveway.

"You mean the..."

Annie shot him a resolute glance. "Right. The hairs. The new you, God save us... and the whole caboodle. Just cool it."

"You've got your religion. Why can't I have mine?"

"Don't get funny! I'm holding you to it. Come on, let's go."

At the front door, Adam turned. "Okay, since you're making all the calls, you ring the bell."

She did. And almost as fast, Adam was standing there, asking himself what these two grinning people, looming before him in their open doorway, could possibly be so happy about. Might they be harboring a secret expectation? Did they intend to quiz him on some personal medical matter? Or was Ed just setting to broach a new investment opportunity?

Looking more closely he could see that Susan was

carrying a lot more weight than usual and Ed had gone the other way. He'd thinned down so much Adam's first guess was some kind of a chronic disease, maybe even one that had required chemotherapy. Especially because Ed had been balding only slowly. Now, he had hardly any hair at all. On the other hand, there was what looked like a healthy enough new growth of mustache. Was it just to divert attention from what what had been lost on top?

Adam leaned forward to get a better look at the fresh sproutings on Ed's upper lip, the while nursing a faint hope that what had been growing there might at least have the good grace of obscuring that which ordinarily bristled from above. No such luck. The damned nasal hairs dangled as always.

The exuberant couple were as one in their glee, Susan in particular.

"Come in, come on in! Great. This is simply marvelous! Sit yourselves down. Well now, what have you two been up to? But first, how about a drink? Annie?"

"Just a little vermouth, if you would."

"Terrific! Adam?"

"Any old scotch, straight up is fine."

Ed demurred.

"Not for you, old buddy. For you, nothing but twenty-five-year-old single malt!"

Adam came on so fast, Annie wasn't sure she'd heard him.

"Hey Ed! Why don't Susan and I fix the drinks and you can get to finish your shaving?"

He reached across to tap an especially discerning fore-finger against Ed's left cheek.

"I guess we rolled up a little too early, old man, and

rushed you through your shave. Didn't we though? You've got a spot, right about there, which your razor never touched. In fact, I think I can also see where the shaving cream's gotten dried up and sorta caked."

Ed appeared flabbergasted.

"Really?"

"Would I kid you? I wouldn't have said a word except I know how fussy you are about appearances and things like that. And while you're tidying up..." He could sense Annie stiffening. "It looks like there's a little lint, or maybe a thread, or some hairs or whatever, hanging down right about there."

Adam pointed straight at the bottom of Ed's nose.

"I'll be damned!"

"Go and see for yourself. Check it out."

Ed took off for the stairs. "Be back in a jiff."

As Ed raced off, ever smiling Susan called over her shoulder to Adam now busy with the drinks.

"How about me, Adam? Do I pass muster?"

"Well I know that thin is out again. But don't you think you're carrying your new you a little too far?"

Annie threw herself into what could become an awesome breach.

"Listen Susan, Adam's being simply terrible these days. Don't mind him at all. For some reason I just don't get, he's decided to needle everyone, and not only tonight. It started up long before we even left the house. Don't pay any attention to his nonsense! You look just fine. And tell me, where on earth did you manage to find that lovely lace shawl?"

Susan seemed not particularly appreciative of Annie's intercession. Her glow was gone. She was readying herself for something.

"Picked it up in Toledo," she hissed. "It's hand-made Spanish lace. I just love it. Bought it in a flea market. I guess we really lucked out."

Adam, drinks in hand, moved in from behind.

"Which Toledo's that? Toledo..."

Susan, now steely eyed, popped off with just the right rejoinder for someone inhabiting Adam's bold new world.

"Okay, Adam, are you merely joking around? Or have you decided that tonight you're going to be an out and out son-of-a-bitch?"

Adam took to a chair directly in front of the two women who now occupied a couch.

"Hey Sue, that's uncalled for. I was only speaking my mind. What's so wrong about that?"

"I got too fat. Right?"

"Well isn't it obvious?"

"And you really don't know which Toledo? You're wondering, maybe it's Ohio?"

"Oh c'mon Sue. Don't make it a federal case. It was a joke. One that simply popped into my head. That's all."

"And the hairs in Ed's nose? They bug you too. Right?"

"Aha! So you've noticed them also. And they don't bother you?"

"No."

"That's amazing!"

Susan, after a deep breath, had at him with a vengeance. "Look, buster. The only amazing thing is that feeling the way you do, you accepted our invitation for dinner."

"It was entirely Annie's idea."

Ed bounced back into the room.

"Hey Adam! You need glasses or something? I looked in the mirror and didn't see a damned thing."

Susan pulled at Ed's sleeve.

"You've got hairs hanging outa your nose that plain disgust him."

Ed was taken aback.

"You're kidding."

It was Annie's turn to say something. But fence mending was no longer feasible.

"Look guys. Nothing good can come of this. Adam's decided, for reasons beyond me, to let go with the uncensored workings of his mind. He's become, all of a sudden, what you might call a nonpareil honest Joe. Which makes him, for my money, a pain in the ass, and certainly not the sort of person most other people would really want to break bread with, tonight, or for that matter, any other night. So before things turn any more sour than they already have, we're gonna' get going. I'm extremely sorry about all of this. But there's just no fixing it. I know you mind. We all of us mind, except possibly Adam. But there's no choice for us except to say good night and to beat it."

On the way home she neither looked at him nor spoke. Once there, it was "I'm going to bed. I'm not hungry. You'll find whatever you might want in the fridge."

"All this over a couple of hairs?"

"No, over not being sure whom I'm living with any more."

For an instant, he saw old plaster and decrepit green paint falling from his bedroom walls. Thank God! He was still immune to it and not bothered at all.

"You could be right. When I got up this morning it was like being treated to a fresh start. I was through the worst of something, a sort of crisis. Like a fever had broken.

And the world had become a real strange place. I could hardly recognize my own bedroom. Especially since all of a sudden it was where anything inconsequential was not to be fretted over any more. And also, here's the kicker, there was nothing that rated being devious or secretive about, either."

His erstwhile loving wife turned on him.

"Or sparing about? Right? What are you trying to stir up?"

"You think I'm just trying to provoke you?"

"Not only me! Everyone else! Look at me, Adam! What can you possibly be thinking?"

"You mean, right now?"

"Sure. What's going through your head? What are you really up to?"

"Up to? About that, I dunno' quite yet. But what I'm thinking at the moment is... well, you've got wrinkles that didn't used to be there. And I see a few little hairs on your chin and upper lip that could stand tweezing. Also, you've become quite gray. But your essence, the thing that drew me to you right from the beginning, that's all still there, every last bit of it. So I can never leave you. Or bear to be without you. And when we have sex, even if it's not what it used to be, so what? I remember the good old days and I fantasize. For my money that's all I need. How's that grab you?"

"Anything else?"

"I was wondering why you break more wind than you used to. It's not too pleasant, especially at night when we're in bed together."

"So from now on this is how it has to be. Right?"

"Has to be? Look, it's not a compulsion. I'm sure I could

revert and hold back. It's simply that for some strange reason it's much easier for me to be honest than to lie a lot. Or maybe the only thing that's going on is that I've finally run out of steam. Maybe I'm just too old to muster up all the creative energy you need to be a first class liar, or even your average every-day conniver. But then again, it could be that I've gotten myself inspired somehow."

"Why would you want to hurt someone with whatever pops into your head and also wind up looking ridiculous?"

"I'm damned if I see how that follows. And why does there have to be all that sensitivity? And all the phony image stuff? Is it that we're only where we are because if we didn't deceive one another for all these years we couldn't have made it. Becoming out and out tricksters was what it took to pull us through? And now, finally, what's actually real is too bitter a pill to swallow? Christ! We've wound up with no taste for how things actually stand!"

"Like I said, I hardly know you any more. I'm awfully tired and I'm going to bed. Maybe with a little luck you'll be your old self in the morning."

Adam watched as Annie, looking drawn, slowly pulled herself along the bannister and made it up the stairs. Some stuff! Best day he'd ever had and she'd just as soon there'd never be another one like it.

Six

Annie didn't get her wish. Things went unchanged, Adam drawing more and more notice for his new ways.

One evening, eight months later, the presence of someone at the front door was heralded by Willy's furious barking. Hearing the sound of a loud knock, Adam led a very resentful dog to the rear of the house and then opened to a tidily dressed fellow holding a brown envelope.

"You Doctor Merritt?"

"Far as I know. Who are you?"

The man didn't say. In any event, it would have been irrelevant.

"I'm supposed to hand deliver this here letter to you. Mind signing for it right over here?"

"What's this? Some kind of a subpoena?"

"Nope. They just wanna be sure you got it."

Adam complied and just as quickly, whoever he was, the man was gone. Annie, hearing the front door close, released Willy from the back kitchen and called out.

"Who was that?"

"Damned if I know. And if your crazy dog doesn't stop grabbing for this envelope I'll never find out."

Willy had a passion for most kinds of paper. Napkins, paper towels, newspapers, letters, even cardboard boxes, were no challenge to the fierce workings of his jaws and intestinal tract.

"Jesus Christ!"

"Now what?"

"What do you mean by that?"

"Well, these days, I never know what to expect from you."

"The medical society wants me to come downtown next week and answer a few questions. It seems that some of my esteemed colleagues are ticked off about how I do business."

"For instance?"

"They don't say. You want to know something? I'm not going anywhere near that place without a lawyer in tow and maybe also one of those court reporters who take everything down. I'm willing to bet they're on some kind of a fishing expedition and looking to nail me for something or other."

"Well, what have you been up to..."

"Now? Let's not hesitate to say it. Let's not leave out your favorite N word. As far as I know I haven't been up to a damned thing. Why do you necessarily assume that I'm getting into one thing after another? And that all of it's got to be bad news? Hell! I'm much more up front and by the book than most other guys around here."

"That could be the problem."

"What?"

"Forget I said anything."

"Listen! If ever there were some kind of a general understanding about what was really true, and if we fully shared our thoughts about it with one another, this world would have to come to a dead stop. After all, what would be left of its mystery? And why should anyone bother to go on? So along came the obliging words for everything that never quite fit, and people started seeing to it that they not only lived, they damned well thrived off of one another's lies. Should an honest Joe come along, it's no surprise they'd register their disapproval and come after him like gang busters."

"They?"

"Okay. You and them. The enemy camp. The wife who just won't buy into what her man is all about and the guys who sent me this letter."

"You're a real charmer, you are."

"Thank you, sweets."

"And you're not only beginning to sound like a broken record. You're scaring the hell out of me."

"You mean like Satan be gone?"

"No. Like you're acting absolutely paranoid. All the medical society probably wants is to know why you haven't been going to meetings or keeping up with your committee work."

"Wanna' bet?"

"And I think it's downright silly to assume the very worst and hire some lawyer."

"Look. It says right here I'm to `answer certain questions regarding a failure to observe appropriate practice parameters.'"

"You didn't tell me that."

"Well what I said was that some of my buddies must

be complaining about me. I just put two and two together, that's all. Anyway, sooner or later it was bound to happen."

"What was?"

"The struggle between good and evil."

"Good God!"

"God has nothing to do with it. And who says that He's so good? For all we know He's taking sides with the medical society."

"Adam? Do you think that maybe you read too many philosophy books?"

"Not really. In fact none of that stuff even registers with me. I only go for it if I want to doze off in a hurry. It's a helluva' lot better than some pill. Anyway, these days I'm more into Henry Roth. Did you know he may have been making out with his sister?"

"Spare me!"

"You too? Harold couldn't take it either."

Adam phoned Irwin Cantor, a lawyer friend who was all for Adam's strategy but who also suggested that a request be made of the medical society for information as to who had actually registered the complaint and what the specific charges were.

Over the next few days, in spite of making several calls to various officers of the society, Adam could get nothing out of them. The last one reached was a Doctor Joe Cannon, the treasurer.

"Just come on down. It's probably no big deal."

Seven

The following Thursday at 2 PM, Adam, Irwin, and court reporter Mary Dickenson entered the outer offices of the Richmond Medical Society. Adam approached the reception secretary and identified himself.

"I'm Doctor Merritt."

"Everybody's here and waiting, doctor. Are these other people with you?"

"Right. He's my lawyer and this young lady is going to take everything down."

With that, the young woman looking a bit askance, got up and headed for a nearby doorway.

"I'll be right back."

Almost at once, Doctor Joe Cannon, who'd been the last officer of the society to speak to Adam, burst upon them from out the same direction. Quite obese, he waddled up looking frantic and ever so put upon.

"What's all this, Doctor Merritt? What's with the lawyer and the stenographer?"

"I just want to have a reasonably accurate record of the proceedings. And if there's going to be some kind of an action against me, sooner or later I'll be needing a lawyer, anyway, so I might as well have the benefit of counsel now. You guys don't intend to say anything you wouldn't want on the record, do you?"

Cannon got real huffy. "Of course not."

"Or to claim I said something which maybe I really didn't? And insist I incriminated myself, the whole thing being a matter of what you all might swear to down the road a piece? And all that happening for lack of any record of the proceedings?"

Cannon didn't see it that way.

"My God, what an imagination you have. And is this what medicine has finally come to?"

Adam needed clarification on that one.

"Medicine?"

"Why sure, old man. We doctors used to be like good neighbors with one another. When we had a problem we'd sort of talk it over, work it out amicably. You know, like over the backyard fence. That's what good neighbors always do. They don't need lawyers and stenographers and needless worries about what simple little misunderstandings might lead to."

"Is that what this is, a simple little misunderstanding?"

"Well Adam, why don't you and I, by ourselves, just go on inside and find out."

"You know what this is all about?"

"Sure."

"Well then tell me what's up, right here and now, in front of Irwin, and I'll decide on what to do."

Cannon got back on his high horse.

"I'm not privileged to do that."

"Then it's the three of us or nothing at all."

"Very well, come on. The bunch of you. I'll send for extra chairs."

It was a formal setting in what appeared to be the society board room. There was a conference table and along one side of it were seated four well suited out men whom Adam assumed to be the president and other current officers. Hanging from the wall behind them were framed pictures of past presidents of the society, each offering a remarkably similar posed smile. There was not a stern face among them. Rather, the dour looks were coming from the presently seated officers looking at him with barely contained suspicion across the intervening table.

Before any of them could utter a word, Irwin, in a rather soft, but persuasive voice, explained that he was there at Adam's request and that whatever the reason for this gathering, it was somewhat irregular for his client to have been summoned in such a manner, all of his requests for information having been rejected.

"After all", he finished off, "how can Doctor Merritt be prepared to discuss questions of patient care if you gentlemen refuse to at least give him the names of the patients involved so that he can review his records?"

The smallest of the officers gave an immediate response. He was dressed in a three-piece, pin striped suit, sporting a gold Rolex, and was wearing Ben Franklin glasses which rested precariously on the tip of a rather severely downturned nose.

"I'm Roger Scott, the president of this society. He doesn't need to look up any records. All he has to do is tell us whether or not he's actually been saying the things he's reported to have said about his fellow dermatologists."

Adam cut in.

"Like when?"

The president was a real quick responder. "Like almost invariably when you get patients who've been treated by other dermatologists, and you happen to disagree with how they've been cared for. More often than not, it's been your recent habit to come right out with claims that the other man is not only guilty of clinical error, but also has some kind of ulterior motive, or vested interest, dictating the manner of his treatment."

Adam could be just as nimble.

"Well, just sitting here, without even looking anything up, I can easily recall certain instances when treatment was so egregiously off the mark that one could draw no other reasonable conclusion."

The president, clearly satisfied with having gotten Adam's confession so quickly, went on.

"Would it surprise you to learn that some of your own patients who went on to consult with a few of your colleagues, reported to them that they left your care having had it actually predicted by you that it wouldn't be too unlikely for them to fall into the hands of doctors who would treat them with few if any scruples?"

"It could happen."

"I asked you if it would surprise you?"

It was time for Irwin to get his own two cents in.

"With all due respect sir, what might or might not surprise Doctor Merritt is not a proper subject for a proceeding of this kind. And as a matter of fact, at the present moment, the only proper issue of surprise resides with your conduct of the matter at hand. In other words, the issue of surprise rests with the entirely inappropriate refusal of you gentlemen to tell Doctor Merritt in advance of today of what he stands accused, and who might be his accuser."

Adam liked Irwin's legal style but preferred his own. "Hey, Cannon. Is this how good neighbors talk in their backyards? It's beginning to look more like a barnyard full of roosters to me."

He turned to his stenographer. "Now Mary, don't you miss a word of this. You get it all down."

Doctor Scott proudly ignored the two of them. "A single physician has registered this complaint. But he has collected more than a dozen statements from colleagues of yours. I'm sure that you are acquainted with the chief of dermatology at Eastern University, Doctor Garrett Swenson. As far as we in this organization are concerned, he has impeccable qualifications and indubitable credibility."

Adam had a different opinion of the "impeccable" doctor. "That guy? He's a bare-faced crook and if I have to, I'll prove it!"

Irwin came back on fast and loud.

"Gentlemen. I have to have a few private words with my client."

He took Adam by the sleeve and rushed him back out to the waiting room, leaving the stenographer behind.

"You out of your mind? You can't just pop off with a statement like that. Especially when it's all being taken down verbatim. Jesus! Having that stenographer here could prove to be your undoing. Because right now she's sure serving those guys a helluva lot better than she is you and me. And what the devil were you jabbering about? Mind letting me in on it?"

"I know all about this guy Swenson. He's the chief of my department. And get this. For putting in no more than ten minutes a week at Municipal Hospital, because all he does out there is sign off on patients' records, he's pulling down a hundred and sixty thousand dollars a year. That's what the city's paying him. Officially, he's heading up their dermatology program. But what he's really doing is taking himself a fifteen minute ride each week so as to cash in on a gravy train. There's a full time resident and a physician's assistant at Municipal who are doing all the work."

"How do you know this?"

"The physician's assistant gave it to me straight. She had some training with me a couple of years ago and I bump into her from time to time."

"Okay, but why is Swenson spearheading this thing? You been bad-mouthing him along with all these other guys?"

"Maybe."

Irwin, who had approached this matter in a calm and deliberate lawyerly manner, was starting to look a bit frayed.

"Maybe? What the hell's that supposed to mean?"

Adam rested a hand on Irwin's shoulder and presented him with the kind of confidence lawyers aren't really prepared for. Nor, if they're interested in coming up with a winning strategy, was this the kind of intimate revelation they'd particularly want to hear.

"Look. When you shoot straight from the hip and always tell it like it is, things like that are damned hard to remember. It's only when you start making things up, getting complicated and devious, you know, like when you lie a lot, that it becomes important to remember exactly what you've said and when you've said it. When you've got a clear conscience, who needs to remember every little detail of what you may or may not have been up to? Life becomes real simple."

Irwin was beginning to get a handle on what he had let himself in for.

"Yeah? You call this hole you've dug for yourself and what I'm thinking is a kangaroo committee all set to either censure you, or do something even worse, a simple matter? I tell you Adam, I don't like the looks of these guys. I'm thinking they're a bunch of sons-a-bitches and even willing to bet they've already gotten their own legal advice on this thing."

"So what? That's why you're along."

It was Irwin's turn to get real confidential.

"Look man. You just made a maybe libelous statement about Doctor Swenson. And thanks to us it's been taken down and recorded real proper. Whatever you said about those colleagues of yours is perhaps hearsay. But what you just said about Swenson, for damned sure isn't. That bunch of vultures in there constitutes all the witnesses that this guy Swenson would ever need if he decided to sue you. What's more, they've not only got your dumb name-calling bullshit down on the record, but right now should you say anything else, remember this, that stenographer of yours is still set to take down everything. Want my advice?"

"Sure. That's why I brought you."

"Apologize and promise to mend your ways. Say it's all one big misunderstanding. And pray that Swenson doesn't get wind of what you said and decide to sue you. Because he's got all the witnesses he'd ever need, plus, thanks to you, a written record."

"Nuts!"

"Adam! This isn't Bastogne. And those guys are are not the Nazis. They are your fellow physicians. You've ticked them off and they're holding all the cards."

"My conscience is clear. Thanks for the advice but there's not going to be any apology. We'll just go back inside and get on with it. Let the chips fall where they may. Besides, court reporter or no reporter, Swenson'd never have the nerve to sue me. He's not gonna say a word. The last thing he'd want is to have people know about his little scam."

"Then do I get to make another suggestion?"

"Shoot. Just as long as it doesn't include an apology."

"Resign. Quit the society. And do it immediately. The way I read the bylaws, they can only reprimand or censure or suspend someone who's an active member. They've got no hold on doctors not belonging to the society nor any legal privilege to speak badly of them in any sort of a public way. Should they do something like that, they'd be opening themselves up to a court action for big time damages. Inside their private little dues paying club they've got a free hand. But once you're an outsider, they'd have to lay off you."

Adam was enthralled.

"Irwin, you're a genius."

"Don't underestimate me. Come on."

Back inside the board room Irwin started things off.

"Gentlemen, I think we've found a way out of this which should make it easy on all concerned. Doctor Merritt is going to explain it to you."

Adam addressed each officer by name, then hesitated, as if at first not sure of his words. Then they came, short, abrupt and not too sweet.

"Look here, you pompous bastards. I quit! As of this moment I resign. Consider me no longer a member of this dumb society. And if any of you come after me, in so much as any way at all, there'll be hell to pay for it. Furthermore,

I expect to receive a full refund on the unused portion of this year's dues. You remember that, Cannon. You're the treasurer, so see to it. And if I don't get a check in the mail real quick, I'll be getting back to you. Now just to make it all official I'm writing it down here, on the back of the notice you sent me, that I resign as of this date."

He passed the paper to the court reporter.

"This young lady here, our reporter, is gonna sign off on it as a witness. Good. Right there, miss. Thank you. Well then, unless any of you have questions, Irwin and I are out of here."

Doctor Scott had one. He had risen and taken a somewhat threatening stance. It reminded Adam of Willy.

"Doctor Merritt, precisely what do you expect to accomplish with this little maneuver of yours?"

"Read up on your bylaws, chief. You read them real careful like and I'm sure you'll appreciate that it'd be a dumb move for either you or Swenson to pursue your little vendetta the least bit further."

Having delivered his parting shot, Adam strode from the room. Once outside he could hear Irwin, who'd lingered behind, saying a few words to the board members. But in a few moments Irwin was at his side once more as they exited the building. He did not look particularly pleased.

"You want to know something, Adam? You're one helluva diplomat."

"Why should I be diplomatic? Why should I kowtow to those birds? We've got them cold. Don't we? You're not changing your legal opinion, are you?"

"No. But why incite them? Why rub it in? Why not just let it all die a quiet death?"

"It wouldn't feel right."

"Right?"

"Sure. You know. Natural. Feelings need to be natural. That's the honest truth. I think."

"Look Adam. This is all over my head. What the hell are you into these days? You join the Hare Krishnas? This some kind of a cult thing?"

"I haven't joined up with anything. In fact, maybe I've gotten myself kinda detached."

Bewildered, Irwin decided that sticking with Adam was not how to spend the rest of his day.

"If you don't mind, I'll head on back to the office. Want a lift?"

"No thanks. I'm okay. The car's parked around the corner. Christ! I hope the meter hasn't run out. Thanks a lot. I'll let you know what happens."

Eight

It was four o'clock. Annie had been waiting. "What happened?"

"I resigned and that should be the end of it. I don't think we'll hear from them again."

Adam described the meeting and Irwin's strategy for dealing with the situation.

"Well if that's that, what's next?"

"Nothing. Nothing at all. Tomorrow I'll go back to work. But today I'm following your lead and having myself a nice little afternoon nap."

"Good for you. You must be exhausted."

"Not really. When you've a clear conscience..."

"I know, I know. Spare me."

Once upstairs, Adam switched on his bedside stereo, expecting to hear some music while changing. But a few minutes later, and still half undressed, he realized that no sound was coming from it.

It must be on the fritz. What to do?

Remembering he had another one, he turned to a dusty old tube-powered set resting on top of his dresser. Betty

Tarrington, a friend from his early Bellevue Hospital days, had left it in his safekeeping almost thirty years ago. Could it fill the bill? Not likely. After all, it had sputtered badly only recently when he'd tried warming it up. But it was worth a try. What was there to lose? Especially since just turning it on had always given him a certain pleasant feeling.

Reaching for the front of its venerable brown bakelite cabinet, he swiveled the on-off knob and felt a hesitant click. Nothing. He sensed it might have hummed briefly but then had become deathly silent. Swinging it around so he could investigate the innards of this ancient contraption from the rear, he saw that all of its old electron tubes were glowing. Odds were that some condenser or maybe a transformer had finally gone bad. So there'd be no music. After pulling down the window shades he got into bed.

Good old Betty, Betty Tarrington. Where the devil was she now? Right now, at that very moment? He hadn't had a word from her in all these years. Was she still over there in Switzerland and married to Eric? Who might know something like that? And this fool radio of hers. Why on earth had he held on to it for so long? And so faithfully? It was a damned crazy thing to do. And especially to keep it right there on top of his bedside dresser.

It hardly made any sense. Even when nearly new, it had never put out even half-way decent sounds. It was no more than a low-fi piece of audio junk from that now defunct electronics chain called Lafayette Radio. And anyway, if somehow after all these years, Betty did turn up again, she couldn't possibly want it back. Not now, what with its present condition and all the better stereos that were out there.

Hell, if she were to actually reappear, she'd say he was plain nuts for hanging on to it for so long. She'd come right on out with it. Betty had always been that kind of a frank, outspoken gal. That's how he'd always remembered her, every time he chanced to see that radio of hers perched next to his bed, on top of the dresser.

Good old up-front, straight from the hip, Betty. Some kinda gal she was. Anyway, lucky for him it was only this small radio she'd stored with him. Her big and bulky stuff, like the skis and golf clubs, all of that had been shipped back to the little town in California where she was born--Sierra Madre. Adam would never have a problem remembering the name of that town because Humphrey Bogart once starred in a movie called *The Treasure of the Sierra Madre*.

Then off she'd sailed to Europe, on a freighter, no less. Often he wondered if once she got there, she'd ever really managed to keep up with her medical training as she'd planned. Or did she just become an ordinary housewife after getting married to that Eric guy she was forever talking about.

For sure he'd heard all about Eric the very first time Betty and he had happened to sit together during a late night meal in the Bellevue cafeteria. She was a first year resident on medicine, he a lowly intern. No sooner than their conversation had begun but she'd let him in on all of the essentials. It seemed that Betty had met Eric while they were students in California and she couldn't wait to join up with him again, over in Switzerland, as soon as she'd completed her current year at Bellevue.

A week later, Adam ran into her again while taking a walk behind the hospital. He'd needed a breather from his medical labors and found her sitting on a bench down by the East River. He could recall her exact words.

"Okay, Adam. Come on. Take a load off. But don't get any fancy ideas. Remember, I'm a promised woman."

There was no mystery here. She never held back, always let everything hang out.

So in a roundabout way, they'd wind up together for hospital-based meals and took in in a single neighborhood movie, the name of which he couldn't even remember, and on the day before she sailed, the one on which she entrusted him with her precious radio, they went on an outing. It was just a visit to the Metropolitan Museum of Art followed by a somewhat bittersweet walk in Central Park. She was wearing a white blouse and rather trim looking dark blue suit. That was it. Kind of sad, from his perspective. Both then and now.

Adam was now in a mood for something no less whimsical and certainly didn't care, at this particular moment, to read any further of the ribald exploits of Henry Roth. So he reached for a book he'd tried to begin many times before, but had always managed to fall asleep over, after the first few pages. It was Marcel Proust's *The Past Recaptured*. Unlike those other occasions, this time the story held him.

The narrator had started off by recollecting that on a certain morning, upon awakening, he'd imagined that his mistress, Albertine, was there beside him only to realize she could only be so by virtue of "torpid memories" locked within his limbs. For this was not Albertine in his bed, but a different woman. It was Gilberte! Albertine had been dead for a very long time.

Adam was torn. But why should he be? Nothing in

his relationship with Betty entitled him to such memories or feelings. The kind that became locked in the flesh of one's arms and legs. They'd barely ever touched. And yet was she, the dreadful thought could not be set aside, like Albertine, now also dead?

He was unable to let go. One way or another, he had to know! But how? The place, Sierra Madre. The means? Perhaps his telephone. Maybe there was a living relative.

Grabbing for a phone book, he quickly established the appropriate area code. Next, he recruited the long distance operator. She needed more information.

"Tarrington? Don't you have a first name? There are three listings."

Adam charged on. "Give me all three."

A David was his first try.

"Hello. I'm calling Mister David Tarrington."

A girl had answered. "Hold it. I'll get him. Who's calling?"

"Adam Merritt. In Richmond."

Now a man was on. "Hello?"

"Mister Tarrington, my name is Merritt. Years ago I trained at Bellevue Hospital with a Betty Tarrington. Would you be related to her? Because I'd like to get in touch. She was a real good friend. It's been many years and..."

"I'm her uncle but you can't. She's dead. She died of cancer over in Holland. She only passed on a couple of days ago."

This thing was unreal. Or much too real.

"My God! What happened?"

"The word we got is that she was working in some research lab with toxic chemicals and wound up contracting a cancer of the liver. It all came on very fast. She never did get back to the States, you know. Did you ever get to meet her husband, Eric?"

"No. I never did. I'm awfully sorry."

"We all are. She was such a fine girl."

"Yes. She sure was."

"Well that's all I know. Take care of yourself, doctor. It's funny that she never mentioned you. Anyway, here's a phone number for Eric. He's still over there in Holland."

"Thanks."

Adam took the number down, sat on the edge of his bed, and stared at the radio. He wouldn't have to care for it any longer. But should he decide to hold on to it, all the erstwhile comfort of knowing it was hers had been extinguished.

"Were you on the phone? I thought you were supposed to be taking a nap."

Annie had come upstairs.

"I had to check on something."

"Why's that old radio all turned around? You fooling around with it again? I can't imagine that it still works. It's an antique by now. Isn't it?"

"What do you mean 'again'?"

"Well you know. The other night. Remember? When you stayed downstairs so long with Harold? After finally getting up here, instead of going right to bed, what you wound up doing was standing over there in front of your dresser, and playing around with all the knobs on that fool thing. I'd swear it sounded like you were talking to it. You really shouldn't drink any more. You know that? I think that alcohol goes right to your head ever since you've gotten a little older."

"Well did you hear what I was saying?"

"It seemed more like asking then saying. I could be wrong but I think you were just about begging that radio to speak to you. To speak to you in all God's truth or what not. Why don't you just give up on that relic? It's of no real use to anyone and even if you wanted to fix it, I rather doubt the parts are still available."

"I was asking it something about all God's truth?"

"Hey! Is that how this whole honesty trip of yours got started? You're getting religion all of a sudden?"

"You know I don't believe in a God. And if I did, I'd be a pagan. The more gods the merrier."

"That's not what I'm driving at, Adam. I'm talking about this deadly speaking your mind business. And it might just play out that way. Real damned deadly if you want my opinion. So is this whole nutty business from too much to drink and some fool ideas about an old busted radio? Or maybe you're finally finding God?"

"None of the above. And since when does a non-dissembling kind of existence need to mean some kind of divine intervention?"

"Whatever, Adam. Whatever. Look, I'm too tired to deal with any of this right now. And you've had you're chance to nap. I can't help it if you blew it. Now it's my turn, so get on out of here."

Adam put on some clothes and headed back downstairs. Willy, at his side, as ever, looked up wonderingly. What was there to say to him or anyone else about all of this? How confess to a terrible sadness over the death of a woman briefly known and long gone, the strangeness of its timing with his reading of *The Past Recaptured*, and a more than half-felt feeling that none of this could be mere coincidence.

Nine

Fall in love with a dead woman? Wouldn't that be one for the books? But after all, it had been impermissible until now. Hadn't she, straight out, closed the door on it? But what conceivable purpose was there to something so macabre, and worse, so futile?

Adam kept up with his professional obligations but wherever he might find himself... home, office, hospital, clinic, the image of a somewhat stern, and yet attractive, brown-haired young woman, in her white silk blouse and trimly tailored blue suit, persisted.

After several days of such fixation, on an afternoon he usually attended clinic patients at Eastern University Hospital, he turned down a hospital corridor and there she was! Of course it wasn't, but then again, it was.

He'd spotted a young woman resident physician walking directly in front of him. She was in hospital uniform, a white jacket and skirt quite like those worn by female residents at Bellevue. Her brown hair was tied back in a reminiscent pony tail, and even from behind he could see that her eyeglasses were similarly large-sized and horn-rimmed. But her stride was what really did it. It wasn't actually a stride. Rather, much like Betty, she made her forward progress in a sort of waddle. And similarly, in Betty's way, she didn't wear stockings. Her bare and smoothly curved calves topped a pair of loose fitting moccasins, by which, because they sloshed about so, the instability of Betty's gait was all the more wrenchingly remembered.

Adam quickened his stride, to come alongside the woman and see her face. No longer was it his Betty. His Betty had somewhat aquiline features. And her eyes were always softly distant. This face was full rounded, and the eyes though also brown, were keenly focused.

For a brief moment the woman seemed to catch on to being scrutinized. But taking no apparent offense, she smiled, then swerved to board a nearby elevator. He was alone again but straining for other grief-charged remembrances of his brief Bellevue days with Betty.

This was worse than the aftermath of fitful dreams. At least following a dream he could employ reason to counter any bad humors surviving to taint the following day.

But here, to the contrary, he'd become fitfully embroiled in wanting mightily to remember, and even know more, about a woman become a specter. And there was no arguing against it, or reasoning it away. Yet strain as he might, he could generate no further remembrances of Betty.

That's when he hit on the idea of phoning Eric, her husband. As a former fellow Bellevue house-staffer and friend, how suspect could a conveyance of his condolences be? Why should a grieving husband surmise that what Adam really wanted was to hear something, anything, that might jog his memory, or in any other way, further what was now a perverse need to feel closer to this other man's dead wife?

On a morning that he was home alone, Adam dialed the number given him by David Tarrington.

The responding voice sounded Dutch and brusque.

"Hello. My name is Adam Merritt. I'm looking for Eric Bloor."

The voice switched over to heavily accented English.

"Well, you found him."

"Betty and I trained together many years ago and I'm very sad to hear that she's passed on. Please accept my heartfelt sympathy."

The voice became even more gruff.

"Yes? I know you. She told me all about you. So what can I do for you, otherwise?"

"You know me?"

"How could I not remember? You're the one who wouldn't send the radio."

"The radio?"

"Yes, the radio! It was a long ways back but who should forget something like that? Twice she wrote you for it, to please send it over. And nothing from you, not so much as a word. It was yours for safekeeping, not for stealing!"

"But I never got any letters."

"Easy for you to say. But hard to believe when she wrote you not once, but twice. The second time she was begging you for it. I know, I saw the letter with my own eyes. So well she explained everything. About how tough it was for us back then when we were first starting out. We had nothing. Absolutely nothing. Neither one of us with a job. Barely able even to feed ourselves, much less the cats. And all she wanted was a little music once in awhile from that radio of hers. And you! For some reason a spiteful or a vengeful man! If you loved her too, how could you deny her? Just because she married me, instead of you?"

Adam knew he was quavering but could do nothing to stop it.

"Hey! You've got this all wrong. We were just good friends and colleagues and I never got a letter."

Eric pressed on, becoming more accusatory.

"I think not. And you'd better understand, for all your tidy little condolences. From then on, she always resented you and spoke badly of you. How well I remember when even near the end, when all she could do was lie there and be reading her beloved Proust and what he'd said about remembrances, she'd say over and over again that it was high time not to remember, but rather to forget. Especially to forget people like you. Oh, my Betty was an honest one. To her last breath you always knew what she had on her mind."

"Me? She spoke of me? Then? And she was reading Proust?"

"Right. You like that, Merritt? You wouldn't if you could hear what she said. And myself? Instead of a few final sweet and loving words, I had to listen to all that crap. So to hell with you!"

Nothing more. Eric had slammed down his phone.

On this bright and pleasantly warm spring morning Adam's fingers were icy cold. He was beset by unrelenting feelings of severance and rejection. This was far from anything he'd bargained for. A misguided ploy to jog his memory had churned up not new and better, but old and rather nasty, recollections. No sooner had he insisted there'd been no letters, he knew it to be a lie, his first in months, as he recalled how way back then he'd acted horrendously but put it out of mind.

Indeed, as Eric claimed, there were two letters from Betty and he'd ignored them both. Well, not so much ignored them as deciding on his own, that shipping her radio wouldn't work out. It had been his reasoning that not only were European broadcast frequencies quite different from those in the States, but also the electric voltages were twice those utilized here. As soon as she would have plugged it in, it would have burned out. Besides which, what reason could he have had to appreciate how much getting the damned thing meant to her?

He'd told one lie to Eric, and now, to himself, he'd come up with another. Whom was he trying to kid? Frequencies and voltages had had absolutely nothing to do with it. People on both sides of the Atlantic had been using step up and step down transformers for years. What happened was that both her letters requesting the radio had also included mention and repeated discomforting reminders of her marriage to Eric.

But as much as she had seemed to relish the communication of such news, Adam found himself resenting it. Not to ship her radio became all too justifiable by his small minded, way of thinking. And after awhile, the matter became buried, along with his hurt. There were no more letters and the situation faded from his mind. Until all these years afterward, he chanced to reach across his dresser top, tried to turn the radio on, and failing at that, picked up his copy of Proust.

But the Proust, much like the radio, was of her. The

thought could not be set aside. What sort of mortal linkages were these?

Adam had never been superstitious but that did not keep him from wondering what exactly was going on since the bounds of coincidence appeared to be exceeded. Especially he wondered whether any of this was connected, somehow, with the recent changes in his behavior. Was it a matter of his being prompted? Best to set such thoughts aside. Hopefully, in due time, like most other unpleasantries, they'd attenuate.

The problem was that he was feeling guilty. Guilty about her ancient radio and that he'd lied so many times. Lied back then, lied now, lied to Eric, lied even to himself. And he was supposed to have changed.

Ten

Doctor Garrett Swenson was not to be denied. What he was unable to accomplish through the medical society (Adam had stymied that), he resolved to instigate on his home grounds as professor and Chairman of Dermatology.

He fired off a letter to the dean recommending that Adam's clinic privileges be suspended. His argument was that any physician indulging in what he deemed to be "irresponsible criticism of colleagues" was neither a proper role model for young doctors in training nor particularly fit to serve as their instructor. Such a fellow needed to be curbed. Adam got a letter from the dean informing him of a six month suspension. If he wanted, he could have a hearing.

Annie took it harder than he did.

"What will you say to them?"

"When?"

"At the hearing."

"I don't plan to ask for one. Why should I? Why should I have to justify my conforming to the second Principle of

Medical Ethics that's been adopted by the A.M.A., which is, and get this..."

He picked up a copy of an A.M.A. publication and read directly from it.

"`To deal honestly with patients and colleagues, and strive to expose those physicians deficient in character or competence, or who engage in fraud or deception'. How's that for you. Straight out of their bloody mouths. So before I go and plead for some kind of a hearing, and find myself before still another damned kangaroo court that's only gonna be out to get me, I'll take them both to court. I'll sue the two of them for damages. Both that old son of a bitch Swenson and the dean as well. What they're doing is way out of line. I think I'll have another talk with Irwin."

"Oh my God. You're going to sink us for sure."

"Come on, Annie. This hasn't got anything to do with how I make a living. I don't get a dime for teaching those residents in the clinic. I do it for gratis. And meanwhile that damned phony, Swenson, is pulling down a cool six figures for absolutely nothing. Maybe if he knew I've got the goods on him he wouldn't be so quick to try and stick it to me. Talk about `fraud or deception.' Let's just see what kind of balls he's got when the chips are down."

"Adam. Don't talk like that. I don't appreciate it at all. You're not with the boys, you know. And I'm not deserving of it."

"Sorry. Whatcha' think, then?"

"Well if you don't want a hearing, why not just ignore the whole thing? You could take the six months off as kind of a... sabbatical. Couldn't you?"

Again, Adam seemed to be remembering Bastogne.

"Nuts."

"Adam."

"I said nuts, not balls. Look, I can't take this lying down. That's the same as saying they've got justification. Well they don't, and I am not going to be walked on. That's out."

"This is all coming from your total honesty kick. Try and tell me it isn't. How you ever got started on it is more than I'll ever know. Just remember that I warned you. Don't ever say I didn't. I just knew you'd wind up in hot water. Or even worse."

Adam's mind, especially since he wanted there to be no further backslidings, was now so open a book, he found himself blabbering almost incoherently.

"Look, honesty is honesty is honesty. An ethical principle is an ethical principle is an ethical principle. What's the use of having things like that if you don't subscribe to them? Besides which, already today, I've lied twice. Once on the phone and the other time to myself. Somehow I screwed up. I relapsed. And it's bugging the hell out of me. Really, really, bugging me. I sure as hell don't intend to do that again. No matter what."

Annie was set to be no less vehement.

"If you tell me about it Adam, or if you so much as hint at what that's all about, so help me I'll murder you. There. Now you know exactly what I happen to be thinking. And mind you, I'm not fooling any. Other than that little disclosure, I've no intention of playing your weird game any further. I happen to have what I consider to be my very own personal space. I'll be keeping to it. And you'd better see that you respect it."

Adam could barely hear her warning. He was thinking once more about Betty. Christ! But wouldn't it be great to be an intern again? And be back in the Bellevue Hospital cafeteria shooting the breeze with that enigmatic gal? But this time around he would not be put off. No sir. Straight out he'd let her know. He'd tell her Eric was one thing but that damn it, he, Adam, was quite another. And that from the very first, what he'd really wanted to do was to grab her. Then, cold stark reality intruded. There'd never be another time around.

His mind wandering that way, he'd missed the tail end of his wife's last shot at him.

"What did you say? I didn't get part of it."

"I said you're becoming kind of spaced out. You don't want to maybe see someone?"

"Just Irwin. He'll know what I need."

"That's not what I meant."

"I know what you meant. Forget it."

Irwin said he'd need no more, no less, than what any lawyer'd want under similar circumstances.

"So how are you damaged? Lose money? Compromised in some kind of a way as to your professional advancement? Not that I can see. And your medical buddies have handled it all real confidential. The bottom line is that all that's bruised is your ego. And nobody'll even notice if for six months somebody else is supervising those young squirts out there in the clinic. Hell. For all anybody knows you're off to the Riviera or gone to the Congo on some kind of a good will medical mission. Forget it, Adam. The six months'll go so fast you won't even notice it. And next time, smarten up. You know what I mean. Play the game."

Adam was unrelenting. "It isn't a game. It's supposed to be a profession with principles. Adopted principles. And

I was only adhering to them. There's absolutely no reason for me to be disciplined."

"Who you kidding? Only yourself, from where I'm sitting. These guys aren't interested in rules or principles. For them, that's all lip service. They deal in position, image, power, leverage, reputation."

Adam had kidded himself twice, but only about Betty. Once concerning the real state of his feelings for her. And the other time, about what were, in all truth, his means-pirited reasons for denying her her precious radio.

"You're wrong. I haven't done anything like that in a long, long time."

Irwin sensed his would-be client was somehow slipping.

"Come again?"

Adam came back on course.

"I'm not kidding myself. I'm just practicing medicine consistent with sound and proper medical ethics."

"That could very well be. But for these guys you've become a royal pain in the ass. And like it or not, you've got to live with them. Unless you really want to wind up in the Congo."

"Know some other lawyer who'd take my case?"

"Come on. What case? You haven't got any."

"Suppose we go to the board of governors of the A.M.A.? After all, it's their bylaws I've been following."

"And what would you have me do before those esteemed gentlemen? See if I might provide justification for each and every time you've badmouthed some other dermatologist during the past year? What a three ring circus that'd be."

"There's got to be a way."

"Hey, get practical. Sometimes there simply isn't."

"Look Irwin, that bastard Swenson is not going to get away with this. By hook or by crook I'm gonna nail him. What it all comes down to is that I'm being penalized, and to my mind humiliated, for doing what's right. Meanwhile, he gets to steal from the till and call all the shots. Maybe I should just tip off someone on the city council."

Irwin was incredulous.

"First doctors and now you're gonna try and mess around with politicians? Spare me. What would they have to do with any of this? And since when would one of those guys give so much as a fart about right or wrong or doing something by the book?"

"Well it's the city's money Swenson's pulling down and stealing. And they're the ones who've signed off on his little scam."

"So all of a sudden they're gonna plead incompetence and embarrass themselves? Get real. Fat chance. Let it go, Adam. Let it all go."

"Well then, how about this? Maybe the state's got some kind of an oversight committee I could get through to."

"Now listen. I've really got no more time for this. I'm due in court in half an hour and need to do a few other things around here before I take off. Let's just put all this on a back burner for the time being. Okay?"

"I'm no quitter you know."

"Tell me about it. But not right now."

Eleven

He'd be his own counsel. Why not? Hadn't he always been somewhat the loner? The only exception was that brief period when there'd existed the possibility of turning his reserved sodality with a like-minded Betty into something other than the tragically destined encounter it seemed to have been. To think about that now was hard indeed. Nor was there a foreseeable remedy for his failing spirits.

Never, what a sorely belaboring word. It dogged him. Never would he set things right. Never might he tell her of his feelings or apologize for having held on to her radio. Never could he change the way she'd collapsed into nothingness, despising him.

These shortcomings of his became a rueful obsession forcing him to think about her more and more, and leaving him unable to forgive himself for having sundered what seemed to him now as having been a kind of vital connection, one with stronger hold on him than he'd ever realized back then. He had to wonder if his old treachery had provided the origin of his becoming no different than all the other money grubbing doctors. And that's how he'd persisted until just about the time she'd breathed her last, and when unaccountably, he'd changed.

So all he had now, aside from these regrets, were patients, a worn out radio, and an increasingly exasperated wife.

One otherwise uneventful day, he decided, quite suddenly, to get it fixed. He had to hear it again. Once more it must sound just like it did in his room at Bellevue when Betty was still alive and sailing her way towards Europe. And most importantly, sounding exactly as it had for her.

Taking care not to cause any further damage, he coiled the radio's somewhat frayed power cord and placed the stilled relic inside a well padded carton. He would drop it off at an audio repair shop on the way to work.

The technician's reaction was not appreciated.

"Why do you want to fix this thing?"

"For old time's sake. Even new, it never sounded like much, but I want to hear it again, anyway. You know. Sentimental reasons."

"When it comes to electronics I don't get involved like that. Whatever grabs you, I suppose, up to a point. So what I need to know right off, is this for whatever it's gonna take? Mind you, mister, I'm not even sure it's fixable. I can't promise anything for something like this until we get it open. And any parts are gonna' be real hard to come by. I don't even know if they're available."

Adam was driven.

"I'm in it for whatever it costs. Just do it."

"Okay. Let's make out a ticket and I'll need a thirty dollar deposit. Ring me in a week."

By some overreaching logic, Adam had an idea that a little luck at the repair shop would provide the next best thing to having Betty alive again, and to being with her. He had no sense of how outrageous this might seem to anyone else.

A week later it was good news.

"Come and get it, Mister Merritt. But it's gonna cost you another sixty bucks."

"Good deal. That's a bargain."

On the day he picked it up, Adam gave the man an extra twenty.

Willy was the only one home so Adam could go directly upstairs and plug it in. It would take a while for it to warm up. From the rear he could see that four brand new tubes were brightly lit. But several minutes passed and not a sound out of it.

Panicked, he began to twist and pull at various knobs. There were six of them. Then, all at once, an uproarious cacophony of static plus the mind deadening beat of very loud gangster rap. Quickly refamiliarizing himself with what were volume and tuning adjustments, he soon had her radio operating properly.

What he hadn't counted on was its old and overloaded loudspeaker putting out nothing remotely similar to what he'd heard in his room at Bellevue. The stations it was struggling to pull in were unbearable. Worse than cheating him out of any genuine kinds of reminiscence, they were profaning the very idea of what he'd had in mind. After all, Betty and he had only listened to serious music. But here in Richmond, classical music stations didn't transmit strongly enough to be within the feeble reach of her cherished radio. And what did come through was terribly distorted.

There'd be another rude price to pay for having stolen it. Because there was only one solution. He'd bundle up the radio and head for New York City.

Twelve

Hardly could he let Annie know he was being way-laid by a dead woman. He said that on the coming weekend he must visit his sister Blanche in New York. She was glad to hear it.

"Well it's high time you set your mind on something other than getting even with that Swenson. It'll be good for you."

"Right. Blanche needs to talk about some money we've invested together. I'll take the Volvo."

New York was an easy drive. It usually took him around six hours and he'd pass the time listening to CDs. His first thought, considering what he was up to, was to put on an old recording of *La Boheme* recently re-released on CD with Richard Tucker and Bidu Sayao as lead singers. It was a recording which had been a shared favorite for Betty and him. He could recall how on certain off duty evenings they'd listened to it together on a scratchy old LP player in the Bellevue housestaff lounge. But now, as he drove along, instead of putting on the CD, he kept his eyes on the road and stared guiltily ahead of him, for the entire trip.

He'd lied yet another time. To Annie. After all, whom had he more reason to deal with honestly, than his enduring wife?

He could not shake loose from that concern until he'd rolled up to the Lincoln Tunnel approach.

There, beyond the Hudson and the Great Bay, the towering buildings of a familiar city rose before him in a glitter. His view of them, magical at first by its abruptness, turned slowly foreign. For this sight was out of keeping with how everything had looked in the old days. Now, there were too many buildings. And all of them stood very much higher. The twin towers of the World Trade Center had usurped what had previously been the low lying tip of lower Manhattan near the Battery. And the Empire State Building, once so dominating, could hardly hold its own now against so many of its engulfing new neighbors. As for Bellevue Hospital? It was not to be seen. Perhaps it lay there somewhere, smoldering forebodingly, lost in the midtown haze.

After negotiating the tunnel, Adam drove up to 59th street through crawling, honking traffic and past motley mobs of self absorbed people. After dropping the Volvo at a close-by garage he checked in at the Essex House. There was only a small overnight bag to be carried so that he could manage, easily and safely, to transport his critical cardboard carton containing Betty's old Lafayette radio. When a bellhop who'd led him to the elevator for the twenty fifth floor had reached for it, he'd quickly brushed his hand aside. Adam had come too far to be taking chances like that with his precious cargo. It was now two in the afternoon.

Not until he'd called his sister to announce his arrival did he look out from his single but generously sized window. Providential, was it? The view it offered was south and east towards Bellevue Hospital. There was time for no more than a brief glance. He had more important things on his mind. First off, the radio had to be removed from its box. That done, and with it resting on a bedside table, he found an empty electrical socket, plugged in the cord and turned it on, at the same time twirling the dial in the direction of WQXR at 96.3, and held his breath. Nothing. Good God, just like in Richmond the first time he'd tried it. Nothing. He'd come all this way for nothing? But after awhile realizing he'd neither advanced the volume nor compensated for a certain degree of malalignment that had always plagued this particular tuning dial, he quickly made the necessary adjustments. And there it was. It had come on. Distorted as always, distantly hollow and chamberlike, with barely any of the essential high frequencies, but yet, quite there. All there. Yes, truly there.

This music. What was it? So familiar. Of course, marvel of marvels. He'd tuned in the Metropolitan Opera live and they were doing *Boheme*. His *Boheme*. Her *Boheme*. Adam's eyes may have welled up a bit as he looked out the window in the direction of Bellevue Hospital. Then, stretching out on the bed, he heard it through to the end.

When Mimi had finally breathed her last, and Rodolfo had screamed her name, Adam knew that once he'd had dinner with his sister, he must head for Bellevue Hospital.

It was ten o'clock when he left his sister's apartment and made for a Second Avenue bus. This was his first bus ride in New York in more than twenty years. It cost him six quarters. Back then it was a dime and a nickel and if you needed it, the driver made change. Now if you needed change, you were plain out of luck. Dare to board a bus without the right coins and you'd be thrown off.

Riding along, he was soon remembering the time he'd been on a First Avenue bus with Betty. Was it when they'd gone to that movie he couldn't recall? Before he could resolve the question, the present bus had arrived at Twenty Sixth Street and it was time for him to get off. After walking east a single block, he stood before the hospital.

Still a dreary sight, Bellevue hadn't changed that much. Not, at least, for what it projected of its essence. New York University had erected brand new parking garages and encircled what could be called the historical sections with a number of towering grey and white clinical appendages. But this oldest hospital of New York City had ministered too long, too inefficiently, and all too uncaringly to the desperate poor, for all of that medical tribulation not to have seeped everywhere and subverted any effort, however well engineered, to cover it up.

Behind the new garages, and in front of the oldest and dilapidated buildings positioned along the East River, were situated what in Adam and Betty's day had constituted slightly newer structures. These were known as the C and D buildings and had provided a front entrance for the rest of the complex. That entranceway was still there. Adam walked through it into a world that looked much as before.

The inside walls were still wood paneled. Lots of seedy looking people were milling about, and an occasional doctor loped past the bank of front elevators. One immediately apparent difference was that these days the female resident physicians were no longer wearing white skirts, nor the men white trousers. White uniform jackets over blue jeans seemed to serve the unisex needs of both, without there being any apparent sensitivity for medicine looking that casual.

Getting on the elevator was reflexic. As was pressing the button for the eighth floor. Those below eight had been for administration, internal medicine, and patients with tuberculosis. What functions they might be serving now, didn't interest him. The important question was whether eight and nine were still living quarters for the house staff. If so, eight should be for men. Betty, along with other female physicians in training, had lived on nine.

Adam remembered that it was only these elevators, the ones for the C and D buildings, which were automatic. In all of the other buildings, G, H, I etc., even for emergencies, one had to wait until some usually surly, city paid operator, commonly aggrieved because of being quite rightly underpaid, finally took it into his head to respond to a doggedly rung signal. It wasn't unusual to see doctors giving up and heading for the stairs. There'd even been times that critically ill patients were hauled up and down flights of stairs in the dedicated and desperate arms of strapping interns or residents.

Arriving on eight, Adam stepped off the elevator, turned left, and looked down a familiarly dismal corridor. The beige floor tiles had been recently waxed but the amber walls, just as before, needed painting badly. He wondered if the sloppy guy who used to run the floor polisher was still around. It was much too long for that, but from appearances, it could be so. Presumably, as in any city building, to do a fast wax and polish was cheap enough, but a decent paint job was considered to carry too steep a price tag.

What struck him next was the smell of the place. He could imagine a yesteryear in which these were still the odors of his living quarters. A bit uneasy, he picked up on a male kind of scent. Sure enough, a few steps down the corridor and to his left lay the wide open doorway to that same large men's room with its white tiling. For old time's sake he made good use of it, flushed the urinal, and moved on.

Right next door, and just as he remembered it, stood the darkly brown enameled door to what had been his room. He noticed its familiar louvered top section, barely adequate for ventilation, but more than sufficient for admitting each and every disturbing sound from the outside hallway. Could someone be in there? The hour might be just right. Almost eleven. At that time, in the old days, he'd have surely been inside, unless called away for patients, and thinking it high time to head for the basement dining room. Maybe also he'd be thinking about running into Betty. Without hesitating, he knocked.

"Who's there?"

Adam was astounded. Things were all of a sudden, real. He hadn't expected the sound of his knock to be followed by anything other that the silence of so many intervening years. Then, he could have made his still disconnected way back to bus, hotel, the Volvo, and Richmond. But he'd been handed another absurd, next step.

He called into the room through the louvers.

"My name's Merritt. I had this room twenty-five years ago."

The response was robustly skeptical.

"Whoever you are, knock it off and stop kidding around. I'm sick and tired of the juvenile bullshit going on around here every damned night. Grow up and beat it." But in the same instant the door was thrown open real fast so as to catch the presumed prankster. Finding only Adam, a changed response from the room's occupant. "I'll be damned. You're for real."

"It's reassuring you think so. Hope I didn't wake you."

"Hey man, I'm on neurosurgery. We don't ever get to sleep. Every once and a while they let us close one eye for maybe two or three seconds. But listen, come on in and have a seat. You here to kinda reminisce? My name's Arnoldson. Call me Neil."

Neil looked to be in his late twenties. He was lean and muscular, in T-shirt and jeans, with closely cropped beard, hair in a crew cut, and had an earnest look about him. He seemed genuinely intrigued by the late night appearance of this visitor to his cell.

The room looked as if it was never touched after Adam had deserted it. There was the same narrow bed with dark metal head and foot rails, a small lamped table beside it serving as a desk, and up against the table, an arm chair. Another louvered door to the left of the entranceway opened into a closet. Otherwise, there was only the familiar looking wall sink. Still standing, after shaking hands with Neil, Adam pointed at the sink.

"It still drips, doesn't it? Ever leak for you? Leaked all the time for me. After awhile I got my my own wrench and gaskets."

Neil seemed surprised.

"No. It never has. Whatcha know? You must have fixed it real good. You know we could use that kind of talent in the OR. Want to try your hand on something that really leaks, like a bleeder maybe? I bet I get a call in the next couple of hours. Saturday nights around here, it's routine. What do you say? Want to hang in and give it a try?"

"I'm hardly up to anything that tricky. When I left here I went straight to Presbyterian Hospital and have been doing dermatology ever since."

Neil had taken a seat on the edge of his bed. Adam was just standing there before him, but eyeing the solitary chair. Neil caught his hesitancy.

"Come on, Doc. Take a load off. If this isn't something!"

The proffered seat, his old chair, was exactly where Adam had last seen it, and where in his own time it had always been. In front of the table and against the wall opposite his bed. A throat contraction was quickly there to remind him that Betty had sat there the night before she sailed.

It was the only time she'd ever been to his room. But he was on call so he'd invited her. What else could he do? Tomorrow she'd be disappearing. He could see her clearly. She was sitting bolt upright with that ever present knitting of hers. Son-of-a-gun, he'd never bothered to ask what the damned thing was going to be. So how would he ever get to know that now? But give that girl half a chance and she'd always go for those wicked looking needles. Come to think of it, to tote a knitting bag along on a trip to the men's quarters may have been inspirational. It would sure make it all look innocent enough. Wouldn't it though? As if it were necessary.

Boheme so fresh in his mind, he could easily recall it. It was coming from the LP player moved for the occasion, out of the lounge and onto his table. He'd been half reclining, half sitting, propped up by the pillow at the head of his bed. How easy to remember that next moment. Unrestrainedly moved by her and the music, he'd gone from the bed, taken those few short steps to her side, and bending forward, wanted no more than to kiss her left cheek. She was raising an intervening hand.

"Please, Adam. No."

So it was "no." They heard the *Boheme* through. She knitted. He fretted. When it was over she went upstairs to her own floor but was back in a few minutes with the radio.

"Here. Hold on to it for me. And I don't want you coming to the boat."

When she sailed he couldn't even see it from his window. It looked towards the East River. And her boat was scheduled to leave from a Hudson River dock on the other side of Manhattan. He could imagine it though. At the proper time, its stacks trailing curls of black smoke, it would become smaller and smaller until finally enveloped by the distant haze. At such a moment, probably for her, he no longer counted. Her thoughts would be eastward and he'd have pretty much ceased to be. Things he'd hardly ever thought of again were back.

"Come on, Doc. Have a seat."

No longer out of it, Adam sat down in their chair, his and Betty's, now Neil's.

"Thanks. Do you like it here?"

"What's to like?"

Betty had called it a privilege to study there. Anything else was "provincial."

"Well you can't deny the experience or all the opportunities to assume responsibility. Can you?"

"No. But sometimes it's a helluva lot better to be personally supervised and this place is such a physical drag for getting almost anything done that most of the time it's real hard to convince my attending doctors to come in. They'd rather give advice over the phone."

"But the accreditation commission doesn't allow that."

Neil shrugged it off.

"They do it anyway. It's pretty much routine."

"That's awful. Have you ever complained?"

"Not on your life. This kind of residency is too hard to come by. Get kicked out of here and forget it. You're washed up for good. But listen, you feel like grabbing a bite? Around this time I generally head downstairs for something to eat. You know, feed the fires. I'd be real pleased for you to be my guest. And I could show you off to the guys."

It was as if Neil was reading his mind. Or had a handle on the scenario.

"How about the gals? Show me off to them, too?"

Neil winked.

"Why not? There's a few might even turn your head. As you probably know, almost half of us can be quite gorgeous these days. Big difference from your days. No?"

"Well that's right. Women made up less than twenty percent. But I did get to know someone. She wasn't what you'd call gorgeous, but a bit of all right anyway."

"Okay, Doc. Let's take off before they close down."

Thirteen

Still in the basement, hard right from the elevator, was what used to be the house staff dining room--and still was. But nowadays, a cash register stood at the far end of the serving counter and the place was being run as a cafeteria open to anyone who paid. It had made things a bit awkward.

"Look, Neil. When you said guest I thought it would be like it always was. Now I feel I'm imposing. You see, when I interned here we had meal cards. Everything was for free and there were always extra cards around for friends or relatives. So how about you saving your money and letting me pick up the tab."

Neil would have none of it.

"No way. I haven't been out of this place for the last ten days. So I'm loaded."

"Loaded? I'll bet. I got forty-two dollars a month."

"Really? Well things have changed, doc. As a third year resident I pull down more than that every day. So grab yourself a tray and drool in envy. But not in the soup."

There were but half a dozen people on the line ahead

of them so there wasn't much of a wait. As they inched along the serving rail Adam couldn't help but look around him, half expecting to see one or more familiar faces. One in particular wasn't there. Nor anywhere. That's what he'd always done. If on entering the dining room he didn't immediately spot her already at a table, he'd keep an eye peeled both front and rearwards as the tray line made its way. To see her after awhile, one place or the other, was kind of a relief. When she never came, it'd be a downer.

Having selected what he wanted, a chocolate donut and coffee, he followed Neil to a table, all the while unable to constrain himself from searching the room in that same old way. It was an unsullied reflex insisting on its sway. What others might be there to dog him?

Neil had caught him at it.

"Hey Doc, whatcha lookin' for? A ghost or something? That donut all you really want?"

It wasn't too hard to be deadly earnest and truthful on both counts.

"Well Neil, I'll tell you. I took your kind invitation not because I'm actually hungry but because I wanted to relive a special part of this. You're right. And if whom I'm looking for were here, she'd just about have to be a ghost. But I'd rather put it a little differently. Let's just say, more like an angel."

Neil had gotten the point and turned serious.

"Dead, huh?"

"It happens."

"The woman you were kind of hinting at?"

"Right. And quite a doll. Not beautiful by any measure, but a doll. And you might think it peculiar, especially the way things go these days, but just about all of what we had was right here in this dining room. The rest isn't even worth describing."

"When did she pass?"

"A few months ago. But I never saw her after Bellevue. Its twenty years since she headed for Europe and decided to stay. She wound up getting married, worked in a research lab, and came down with cancer."

"Christ, that's awful."

"Yes it is."

Neil was right. Some very good looking lady doctors had filed in and were scattered about at various tables. But none of them were so reservedly pleasant or with that same kind of unfading, half smiling, whimsical look about them.

The subject had been exhausted. What more to be said about a love affair that never happened? Until now. And by that measure, one so bizarre, it was far out of keeping with anybody else's sense of reality.

To say anything more about what had happened back then would only have him for a pathetic, non-assertive, sap. Which left nothing more to be discussed between Neil and him as Adam cared little about neurosurgical or any other kinds of training going on at present day Bellevue. Nor had he much curiosity for what else might be taking place within this moldering pile of grimy red brick.

He'd been in hope of a pleasant apparition. Its failure to materialize served only to drive home his long held impression of Bellevue as an estranged and uncaring place. Nor did this busy medical workshop have any flair for putting on display the memorabilia of those who'd achieved and studied there in ways that were the least bit respectful. The esteem or the affection he himself had harbored over the years for both renowned professors and fellow house staff members, were for this stark and cold place, a conflicting anomaly.

He remained to finish his coffee and chat with Neil and one other resident just long enough to not seem unappreciative. On the way out he barely looked about him. If Betty was anywhere, it wasn't here at Bellevue Hospital.

His return to the Essex House was by cab. No point to wasting valuable time riding buses. He wanted the company of the radio. Once in his room he tuned it to WQXR and fell asleep. At three in the morning it was still going so faithfully, he let it play right through the night.

Checking out right after breakfast, he got to his garage for the Volvo at around nine. That early hour soon found him driving eastward along Fifty Ninth street, prepared to turn south into Fifth Avenue. But a mere instant of reconsideration soon had him pressing on further to Madison Avenue and then turning north, instead.

In a little while he'd parked the car on Eighty Sixth and was walking towards Fifth Avenue and Central Park. It was where Betty and he had walked together the weekend before she left, after taking in an exhibit of Manet paintings at the Metropolitan Museum of Art. At this moment Adam had no interest in the museum. Rather there was a special spot he'd forgotten all about until he had almost turned south and headed away from it.

Now he was standing exactly where they had paused for a short while on the east side of Fifth Avenue opposite the park. He positioned himself, as well as his memory permitted, pretty close to where he had come to a stop back then and turned to have a good look at her. Next he switched over to where she had stood. How curiously she'd stared at him, not at all understanding what he was up to.

At first it had been simply to admire her. Then he'd taken her by the arm and made her change places with him. That way the light was much better. It fell more softly on her face. With his Rolleicord camera quickly focused, before she'd hardly realized what was going on, he'd gotten off two well framed shots. She laughed at him. They started to walk again and crossed Fifth Avenue to enter the park.

"You must send those pictures on to me!"

She'd never asked for one of him. Nor did she offer to take the camera and try to snap one. It had bothered him a lot. But not nearly as much as it bothered him now, a seeming million years later, to try and remember what had ever happened to those two pictures.

It was something to agonize over, all the way back to Richmond.

Fourteen

Back in Richmond at five-thirty, he began to search. He hadn't remembered those snapshots for so long, there were many possible locations. He sorted through the cluttered contents of various wall cabinets, closets, and bureau drawers to no avail, in the process becoming dismayed by this reminder of the number of useless things he'd sequestered for so many years, without the will or discipline to trash any of it. Now he was paying dearly for his laxity.

One further difficulty was that he had no idea of what kind of envelope or other enclosure he'd used to store the pictures.

Annie found him right after dinner, sitting on the couch in the den, amidst piles of old papers, boxes, and faded photographs, as well as dried out tins of tobacco from his pipe smoking days. He'd already been through the wall cabinet in which all of this junk had been stored. Now he was in the midst of a second exploration of the same location. Getting nowhere with it, he was becoming a little desperate.

She pointed at the tobacco tins.

"You plan on smoking again? If you are, let me know and I'll move out."

"Never fear. Besides, all my pipes, even the Dunhills and the Charatans, turned sour a long time ago."

"Then what on earth are you doing?"

"I'm just looking for a couple of pictures."

He hoped that would be the end of it.

"Of what?"

"Whom would be better."

She was obliging.

"Okay. Of whom, then?"

"Well when I was up in New York I stopped by Bellevue Hospital for a look-see and was reminded of people I knew back in my training days. One resident in particular."

So far, it was a perfectly candid representation.

"And those pictures are important enough to tear the whole house apart? Until you got all of that upstairs stuff put back, we were starting to look like we'd just been burgled. Who're the pictures of? Or am I not permitted to ask?"

Now he had a problem. To be further evasive, was not acceptable. However miserable it might make the two of them, he had to be totally open about this. He had no choice. There was to be no more lying.

"They're pictures of a woman. I think I was more fond of her back then than maybe I appreciated at the time."

Annie took it in amazing stride.

"So where's this doll now?"

"She's dead."

"Oh. Well, in that case, carry on. And if you do manage to find her picture, I want to see it. I'm curious about who you went for in those good old days. But for God's sake, don't wreck the place any more than you have to while you're poking around. Nice having you back, Adam. But you know? It's sure getting weirder and weirder around here." Annie headed back to the kitchen. It could only be a reprieve. Eventually she'd have to know the whole story. The only thing holding him back from following after her, and spilling it right then and there, was that he was locked on finding the pictures. He couldn't bear being sidetracked as much as a minute for anything else.

What to do? How many times could he hunt through these same places? But there were no others he could think of. Disgustedly, one by one, he began to stack this particular horde of relics back inside the cabinet where they'd been buried for years.

Starting at the rear of the lowest shelf, he laid the envelopes down first, placing them, one by one, on top of another. As he did, his finger happened to touch something at the back of the shelf. It felt like a piece of cardboard but he couldn't be sure. He went for a flashlight and pointing it toward the rear of the cabinet, all at once it was a happy damned day.

A small manilla envelope, immediately looking very familiar, could be seen to have slipped down into a crack between the wall and the very back of the shelf. Descended another quarter of an inch, it would have been gone forever. Not only would he have failed to recover the Kodachrome slides, but her last letter to him would have been lost as well. It had been stored in the same envelope.

How gratifying to be disburdened. Even without opening the envelope, he knew what he had. Because now, he could remember having hidden it there. He had only to abide the few minutes it would take to dump everything else back inside the cabinet so he might begin to examine his precious mementos.

First, the two Kodachromes. He selected one and held it before the light of an adjacent table lamp. Betty was looking so familiar. So intimately recognizable. Amazing, and so alive. But he'd been quite wrong about one thing in his recollection of that last day. It wasn't a blue suit she'd had on, after all. It was a lightweight coat she'd worn. And by the looks of this Kodachrome slide, the coat, a navy blue one, was unbuttoned, making it possible to see her dark skirt and a white silk blouse.

Looking more closely, Adam could make out a blue leather bag being squeezed against her side by the right forearm. Also, sticking out of a coat pocket, into which she'd dug her left hand, there was a folded program for what had to be the art exhibit they'd just been to at the Metropolitan. If only he'd kept a copy for himself, what further reminders there might be. The more he thought about it, it was reasonable to assume he might have done just that. Not reasonable enough, on the other hand, to forage through the house once more, only to invite Annie's belittlement or further accusatory comments regarding a suspected determination, on his part, to destroy the place.

Now he was looking very closely at Betty's face. Her gaze was off to the left and she was struggling to smile through a moderate squint. He must have posed her directly into the sunlight, after all, because she seemed to be laughing at the awkwardness of what she was being put through.

Raising a magnifying glass to the Kodachrome, he hoped for at least a glimpse of what he remembered to be her soft brown eyes. No use. Too much of a squint. She was laughing at him for trying the impossible.

Then the other slide and there were two things about it. First, her left hand was now drawn from the coat pocket and was being pressed against her hip. Pressed hard enough to give the hand a prominent retroflexion and to indent the coat in a way that intimated the underlying presence of a provocative curvature below the waistline. But secondly, her face. Either she'd decided on her own and he had happened to catch it just right, or she'd been instructed to look straight into the camera. For here was a head-on, warm, and ever so affectionate smile directed smack at him and there were those brown eyes, so gentle and so brown as it took no straining at all now, to fully remember.

Regrets. Sweet but hurtful regrets, prompted by the second Kodachrome. Was it not reasonable to suppose that at least for that one moment she cared for him? And he, idiot that he was. He was so caught up in focusing or otherwise fiddling around with his dumb camera, that he'd plain missed it. He never saw that look on her face.

It had taken twenty odd years for him to catch on to the sad fact of a lost opportunity to initiate the natural, the appropriate, the spontaneous embrace, that the situation fairly cried out for. And maybe, just maybe, on that sunny and fragrant spring day, who's to say what might then have happened? A kiss? Dare he also imagine a kiss? What would it have been like? What would have been the feel, the taste, of her lips? What kind of sensation, the press of his body against hers?

Adam laid the Kodachromes aside. He no longer needed them. Images of a Betty alive were now fixed and working. And in no way could they be reconciled with the certainty of a Betty dead. He rebelled against such thinking. All the more so, because now he read her last letter to him.

She was "delighted" to hear how well things were

going for him. And she was struck by the peculiarity of his having written of "the hopelessness of getting all the good breaks." Which was something he neither recalled, nor what precisely he might have meant to convey by such a statement. He stopped to think about it, but all he could come up with was that to finish his training, secure specialty certification, and nail down a clinical post, all constituted rather boring and far-gone certainties to his confident way of looking at his situation back then. Or had he been intimating that all such prospective, so-called good breaks stood for very little in the face of her being married and absent?

But then, here it came. The real basis for her letter.

"When will you send me my radio? I could really use it now, what with all the free time I have for music and reading. By the way, I'm having quite an experience with Proust's *Remembrance of Things Past*. Such really marvelous style! And just like he says, Adam, fragments of the past do manage to remain even if the whole is gone, except for what is relegated to our memories."

Other things she wrote about were Eric and his "wretched cats," the difficulties in finding a research job, and compared to New York City, the "provincial character" of medicine abroad. She closed with "All the best to you, Adam. As always, Betty."

"As always"? As always he'd be damned, accursed. For he could see her on her dying day, changed to hating him, because he'd never sent the radio.

Even with what he was going through these days, so much was he also being reminded of her, what was there to surmise other than that there might be a connection with his dereliction?

Fifteen

Willy was acting strangely. He no longer trailed after Adam and had taken to eyeing him suspiciously, even growling at times when Adam entered rooms he happened to be asleep in. The dog appeared not to have picked up on Adam's initial make-over. At least there'd been no overt change in his behavior at the time. But since Adam's return from New York City, it was as if Willy sensed some kind of unfamiliar or objectionable presence whenever Adam and he were in the same room together. Annie caught on to it right away.

"You're gonna have to stay out of this kitchen when he's having his lunch."

"You kidding me?"

"No, Adam. When you're around he stops eating. And I haven't got all day for feeding him."

"Maybe he's got something wrong with him. I could take him to the vet."

"It's only when you come in."

"Great, that's just great. Now even my own dog has it in for me."

"Oh come on, don't get paranoid. Maybe you're using something different, like a new cologne, or a deodorant he doesn't care for."

"Not true. I should smell the same as always. But I did read once that in certain breeds, I think it was Great Danes, the male dogs can turn real ugly with just about everyone, even their masters, once they turn three."

Annie was relieved to hear it.

"Well as long as he stays in love with his mistress, this dog's got a home."

"Even if he starts tearing me apart?"

"Sure. What could Willy do that'd be any worse than what you're managing to do to yourself?"

"Now you listen here. It's been months since Swenson dropped me from the clinic roster and in all that time I haven't had a single run-in with anybody."

"That may be. But all the same, Willy's been acting like you're up to something ever since you're back from New York. And I'll take his instincts over your word."

"Thanks a lot. But tell me something. In a hostile environment like this, how'm I suppose to be the loving and caring man of the house?"

Annie, fifty-three, and although a little grey, was still a buxom, good looking woman. She stepped around her dog, and coming up to Adam, managed to collide her chest and forehead against his. It was done in much the same manner as current among certain arrogant basketball players she liked to watch on TV. Then she kissed him soundly on the mouth. Annie followed all the basketball games. It's what kept her glued to the kitchen television set long after evening meals were over and the dishes had been done. Adam cared little for sports of any kind.

She was proud of how she'd caught him off guard.

"There, how's that grab you? Come on, kiss me back. Make it a dunk."

It wasn't the kind of endearment he'd had in mind.

Nevertheless, he moved forward intent on obliging her. But Willy, who was standing at his dish nearby, growled, curling his right lip to expose an intimidating canine. Adam withdrew.

"Hey boy, what's gotten into you? You think maybe I oughta' try giving him a treat?"

But Willy wouldn't allow Adam to move in the direction of his biscuit jar resting at the far end of the kitchen counter top. He stood his ground and now both sides of his upper lip were curled back, as an ominous rumbling began to issue from somewhere deep in his chest.

"Jesus Christ. What's wrong, boy?"

Annie was all admiring of her dog.

"He's a little darling, isn't he? Now look here, Adam. You're gonna' have to go back inside. Like I just finished telling you. He doesn't like being interrupted when he's eating."

"Right. Tell him I apologize. Will you?"

"Positively."

What a mess. His own dog was turning on him and Annie was making like her favorite basketball players.

Adam retreated to the living room thinking that perhaps a little music would help to settle him down. It was the Saturday following his New York stopover. At first he'd half a mind to hear Boheme once more, but couldn't quite bring himself to do it. That music was much too loaded. Loaded with all those memories he must somehow find a way to get past.

Something else. Maybe Meistersinger. Sure, Meistersinger. Betty and he had never listened to Meistersinger. So if anything could do it, it'd be Meistersinger. And that last act might be just the thing. Turning to his CD player and receiver, he switched them on and inserted the recording. Then he started to search for the proper track. Was it track twelve or track thirteen? Though he'd played that part often enough, it was hard to remember. Anyway his phone had sounded.

"Hey dad?"

Harold. Right now, he didn't need this.

"Don't call me..."

"Yeah. I forgot, sorry. Whatcha' doin'?"

"You mean what was I doing. Don't you?"

"Come on, Adam. Don't be such a stickler."

"Meistersinger. I was going to listen to Meistersinger."

"Don't know that one. Mozart. Right?"

"No. Wagner."

"Coulda' fooled me."

"Well I won't. I give you my personal guarantee."

"Good. So how was the Big Apple? I called after you'd left. Annie told me you were headed up there."

This was awful. How could he bring himself to make a clean breast of things with Harold? The guy was becoming, more and more, such a stickler for the straight and narrow.

"Don't ask me again and I won't have to tell."

"You weren't foolin' around were you?"

"No."

"So then what's not to tell? Come on, Adam, let me in on it."

Adam stopped hesitating. If Harold was going to insist on being a nuisance, he might as well let him have it. He spilled the beans. Every last one of them. Harold must have been dumbfounded because after Adam had finished his account of the previous weekend, nothing was coming from the other end for quite awhile. Finally, he got himself together.

"I don't get it. I really don't get it."

"No one asked you to."

"Yeah, yeah. But I hope you're not trying to tell me you're gettin' to be that kinda' way, like sorta fallin' for something like the ghost of this dead gal you hardly ever knew, but who's maybe passin' you signals from the big blue ranch up there. You're not doin' that, are you?"

"No. I'm leaving you to draw your own conclusions."

"Come on, Adam, break it to me."

"I've done all that the law obliges me to do. The rest is up to you. So bug off on all of this, okay? Now why don't we change the subject? Anything new on your end of things? Otherwise I'm heading back to my Meistersinger."

"I need your advice. That's actually why I called. Both today and last week also."

"Shoot."

"I gave this gal I met about a year ago a diamond brooch. Right away she came back to me sayin' it was worth next to nothing like the three thousand I paid for it. She had it appraised soon as she got the thing home."

"Simple. Tell her to give it back and you'll be glad to return it where you bought it. If she's right you can give them hell. Maybe even get a full refund."

"I'd be too embarrassed to do something like that. And besides, she's so mad at me I don't think she'll give it back. She could've even tossed it out. So what'll I do?"

"If you don't like my idea, suffer. And keep on suffering.

Anyway, from here on in I'm only into ethereal, metaphysical kinds of things. For advice on something like that you need a person who has both feet on the ground. And that'd have to be someone besides me. Bye bye. And take care you don't really shoot yourself in the foot. Remember. This time it's only money. Suppose you married a dame like that. Where would you be then?"

"Don't hang up."

"Why not?"

"I really like this gal."

"So give her a credit card and let her buy whatever she damned well pleases."

"How do I do that?"

"Just call up VISA or American Express and authorize it. They'll send you a credit card on your account but with her sweet little name on it. All you have to do is give it to her or if you really are that embarrassed, you can drop it in the mail."

"Boy, that oughta impress her. No?"

"Absolutely."

"Then what?"

"Well that depends on what kind of a card it is. You know. Standard, gold, platinum."

"It's platinum. I can draw up to fifty thousand on it."

"Look, Harold. Take it from there. But if you give this dame your platinum VISA you are gonna wind up with one helluva problem."

"So why suggest it?"

"I like the idea of not being the only one to make a mess of his life. Listen. I gotta go. Take care."

Would that something like Harold's kind of problem were all he had to cope with. As for Meistersinger, he'd lost his taste for it. He sat where he was, staring at the wall and brooding. Willy, now finished with his lunch, walked past the living room doorway, cast him a non-aggressive but still disapproving look, and then moved on towards the front hall where he could be heard to issue a grunt as he thudded to the floor on top of his favorite oriental carpet.

What did one do in a situation like this? He had this sense of a close by, grudge-filled presence. But no matter how clear he wanted it to be that his inexcusable behavior all those years ago was only about her taking off and getting married, without him having any real chance of doing a thing about it, he saw no way to ever get straight with her about the radio.

Another problem was that Annie was as much of a stranger to him, as apparently he was to her.

Sixteen

The first Tuesday of every month was Adam's turn to lecture the third-year medical students at Eastern University. The following Tuesday found him ready as usual. Customarily, before a lecture, he would check in with the departmental secretary, pick up his mail, and receive the handout teaching syllabus for distribution to the students.

This day was different. The secretary had news for him.

"Your lecture's been cancelled."

"How come? The students have a schedule change?"

"No. Doctor Swenson's giving the lecture."

"What do you mean, `Swenson's giving the lecture'?"

"Look, Doctor Merritt, all I know is what I'm told. That's it. And I'm not getting in the middle of anything."

"When was all this decided?"

"An hour ago. We called your home but apparently you'd already gone. I left a message on your tape. I'm very sorry, doctor, if you've been inconvenienced."

"Where's Swenson?"

"Back there, in his office, pulling his teaching slides."

Adam wasn't entirely sure of why he came to a boil that quickly. He merely sensed an indignation sufficient to propel him right through an intervening waiting room and past the open doorway into Swenson's office.

Doctor Swenson, a gray faced and balding gnome of a man, was bent intently over his upper desk drawer from which he was busily fishing slides for loading into a projector. Adam didn't bother with any of the ordinary niceties.

"Doctor Swenson! Why'd you cancel my lecture?"

Swenson raised his eyebrows, but not his chin. All of his attention remained directed to the contents of his desk drawer. And there was no reply from him until, apparently satisfied he had what was needed for his lecture, he deigned to respond. But not to Adam. He hissed his answer in the direction of the projector carousel into which he'd begun to insert his slides.

"I didn't cancel it. I cancelled your giving it. From here on out, I'll be taking the students on Tuesdays."

"But that's my only teaching day. And I've had it for six years. You've always taken them on Fridays."

Swenson looked up, but still with an avoiding gaze that went right by Adam. He continued to speak, and in a rather smug, self-satisfied way, addressed the bare wall behind his confronter. For Adam, the smirk that played across Swenson's prissy little face was even more annoying than the mean little plot he now chose to divulge and take obvious delight from.

"Correction, Adam. I've got them both days. In the future I won't be using you for lectures."

There were quick twinges in Adam's forearms, legs, and stomach.

"'Using me'? Hey, where do you come off to talk like

that about me? Aren't you forgetting something? I'm a full professor and also a senior member of this department."

But his chief was determined to prevail. Now brazenly aglow, his retort was meanly scornful.

"No use getting your back up. Professorship or no professorship, I'm the one who runs things around here. I've every right to either schedule you for lectures or not schedule you. And as long as you persist in maligning my reputation, as well as that of some other men in this town, fine upstanding professional men whom I both know and respect, you are going to face the consequences. God knows, you may even be unloading your vicious little tales on our medical students. I wouldn't put it past you one little bit."

"What the hell are you talking about?"

By now there remained no more than five minutes before Swenson's purloined lecture, but he was on a roll and keenly ready to oblige Adam with a particularization of his grievance.

"Only yesterday, a patient of mine came in and said that while I was away on vacation she happened to consult with you. Apparently, it wasn't enough for you to simply disagree with how I was treating her. No, not you. You actually had the unmitigated gall to claim my care of her was criminal."

"Would that be Zelma Stevens?"

"Are there others I've treated in a criminal fashion?"

"Christ, I don't know about others. I just know you had that poor lady on high dose steroids for more than six months. You ever hear about putting the adrenals out of business, or intestinal ulceration, or low calcium and pathological fractures? Man, you must be out of it. Absolutely out of it."

"I've had quite enough out of you."

Swenson made an abrupt move to rise from his chair. It wasn't done with menacing intention, but rather to get out of there as quickly as possible. Adam read it differently and decided to counter. He reached across Swenson's desk, grabbing him by his right coat sleeve.

"Not so fast. Let's have this out once and for all, you money-grubbing little crook."

His adversarial nemesis wrenched his arm free and managed to draw backwards in the direction of a rear doorway to his office, but couldn't resist pausing long enough to vent some curiosity regarding this new revilement.

"Damn you, Merritt! What did you mean by that crack?"

Now it was Adam's turn for self-puffery.

"Listen up, mister chairman, when you've been around this school as long as I have, nothing gets by you. I know all about your little scam out at Municipal Hospital. How'd you like it if I tipped off some newspaper reporter about how you've been drawing hundreds of thousands of taxpayer dollars for putting in no more than five or ten minutes work each week? How'd you like that? Hey? Garrett old boy?"

On this quick parry, what little color there was in Swenson's face drained away almost instantly. Adam started to advance upon him again. Now clearly alarmed, and determined to escape as expeditiously as possible, Swenson took a hasty extended step towards his rear doorway. Adam responded with a mock move as if to block him but pulled up short and called after his well-harried and chastened chief as he bolted down the outside corridor in the direction of the lecture hall.

Swenson had been in so much of a hurry to get away,

he'd left behind his projection slides, as well as the student teaching syllabus. Adam held them high.

"Doctor? You want me to send these over to you? You conniving son-of-a-bitch."

At the same time, Adam was deciding that now he'd really have to see the dean.

Seventeen

His run in with Swenson could not be confided to anyone. No point in further exceeding Annie's patience. And Adam was sure that Irwin would only veto his going to the dean or some newspaper reporter. Neither Annie nor Irwin would consider it sound for him, at this point in his professional career, to be making more waves. But this wasn't about making waves. It was about having no alternative other than to put a stop to Swenson. So much for that. He'd do what had to be done.

And as for waves? Two images of them came to mind. Both real troubling. For one thing, they were not to be held back. Canute learned that the hard way. Waves were set to wash over you. To bash you around and drag you down, pull you under, every last time.

He conjured up a wave tossed liner and could see Betty clearly. She had stayed up late the first night of her ocean crossing in order to compose that lousy first letter to him. The letter which was all about Eric and how improbable it was she'd ever get back to the States, but wishing him "all the luck in the world."

Oh but didn't he oblige her? Didn't he wind up having all the luck she'd wished on him? Great luck, fantastic luck! Luck with all of the associated breaks he came to rue and ultimately, to hate. To hate as much, perhaps, as he hated her for that hastily dashed off letter. Why had she been so hard-pressed to set the record straight, yet one more time? Why in such a rush to rub it in? Couldn't she at least guess (no matter that neither one of them fully realized it back then), the extent to which he cared?

So he'd held on to her damned radio. And wound up turning a deaf ear when eventually she'd pleaded for it. The die had been cast. It was only for Eric, all these years later, to drive in the last nail by letting him know how much she'd come to hate him in kind, and much more than full measure.

Waves and hatred. Was nothing positive to come of all this? Not a chance. What he was feeling was only more of the same now that his loathing for Swenson had taken him over.

It took a week to arrange an appointment with the dean.

Adam sat in Dean Miller's anteroom for almost an hour waiting for him to get off the phone. Finally there was a buzz to the secretary and he was ushered in. Miller was the usual kind of ambitious academic who no longer found it interesting to practice medicine, in his case that of infectious disease management, and had directed the sum total of his energy into medical politics and self promotion. Word had it his next step up would be to the university vice president's chair.

Looking always like he'd just left the barber's chair, perfectly groomed and healthfully ruddy, if white haired and solemnly vested, he never failed to direct one of his hollow smiles at whomever crossed his path, even if it happened to be someone like the errantly behaving Adam.

"It's so good to see you, Adam. How's that wonderful wife of yours?"

Adam, day after day, had been waiting impatiently for this meeting. He had no time for small talk.

"She's just fine, thanks. You know what's going on between Swenson and me?"

Dean Miller might also have been considering himself for a diplomatic posting somewhere down the road.

"Well, in a way. But let me have your side of it."

Adam gave his version. From his first inkling that he had a problem by way of the medical society hearing, to his suspension from Municipal Hospital, and now, the cancellation of his lecture schedule.

His dean was real impressed.

"Things have certainly been getting out of hand. Wouldn't you say, Adam?"

It was a relief to hear that the dean was right on target.

"I appreciate your seeing it like that. So you'll straighten Swenson out? And right away?"

But Adam had read Dean Miller wrong, exceedingly wrong.

"Adam, I'm going to let you in on something, and I want you to listen very carefully. I put a lot of stock in respectful professional collegiality. That's where I believe the emphasis must invariably be. And from what Swenson tells me, that's where you've managed to stray and to stir the pot. What you've been saying about other dermatologists, including your own chairperson, is in my opinion inimical to presenting a favorable professional face to our constituency, the sick patients who count on us for the right kind of mien, as well as dedicated care. As for how Doctor Swenson runs his department, that is not for either one of us to say. Not you, and certainly not me."

"Hell, you're the bloody dean!"

Dean Miller decided to take Adam into his confidence.

"Look, Adam. When we think enough of someone to make him chairman, we give him a free hand in the running of his department. Barring issues of unlawful conduct, serious ethical deviation, or some very gross administrative malfeasance, we stay out of it. So if Doctor Swenson has decided on a little thing like changing the lecture schedule, he's entirely within his privilege to do so."

Adam, beside himself, decided to take his best shot. He railed about Swenson's pilfering of city funds from Municipal Hospital.

"You wouldn't call that lawful or ethical behavior would you?"

Dean Miller then began to address him, not as a colleague or fellow professor, but as one might some deviating schoolboy.

"Now don't you really think that's solely a matter for the city government to be concerned with? What could that possibly have to do with us here at the university? And mind you, I've no idea at all if what you say is even true! Now do I? All I have is your word for it. And I feel duty bound to tell you that Doctor Swenson insists that what you've just said, every last bit of it, is utter nonsense. He says he puts in long hours out at Municipal and if necessary, he'll prove it."

Adam, straining for steadiness, went for a more fundamental tack, one better suited to his present needs than possibly having to crawl, hat in hand, before this pompous ass.

"You two are in bed together. That's it, right?"

"I can't imagine I'm hearing this."

He had no recourse but to press his point. Press it to his idea of a logical end.

"Okay. If that's how it's going to be around here, why should I bother any more? I quit. Hear me? I quit. You can take this dumb and presently non-teaching professorship of mine and shove it. Go and give it to some spineless jerk who's willing to look the other way while guys like Swenson, under absolutely no peer review at all, have themselves a free ride, commit malpractice, steal from the public till, and even wind up getting promotions and kudos while they're at it. Hey Mister Dean, how do you like them apples? And how many skeletons might there be in your own closet? Does it bear looking into? Have I been missing something around here?"

"Let's stop all of this right now."

Adam leaned across Dean Miller's desk as if not wanting anyone else to hear.

"Listen up. I'm out of here, and for good. But this is not the end; it's a beginning!"

Eighteen

The next morning, he headed for his office an hour early. Zelma Stevens monopolized his thoughts. It started with Swenson's mentioning of her and had simmered. But when the dean turned lockstep with Swenson, it all came to a head. After pulling her medical records, he looked for her telephone number and jotted it down. Then, closeted in his private office, he dialed her number. She picked up on the first ring.

"Morning!"

"Mrs. Stevens?"

"Yes?"

"This is Doctor Merritt. How are you getting along?"

"Well, not too good. As a matter of fact, I've been meaning to call you. You see, I've gone and fractured my left hip. And now there's something wrong where they did the surgery. It seems they used some kind of a metal pin to hold the bones together but everything's started to shake loose again so I'll have to have another operation. It's a funny thing though. I never even took a fall. That hip of mine just went and collapsed. It broke out from under me while I was going up the stairs."

"I'm very sorry to hear all this but you know I don't do orthopedics. I was only calling to ask if you might be able to remember what Doctor Swenson had to say when you went back to see him."

"Well, I'll be darned. You know that's exactly what I wanted to talk to you about? He was mad something awful, especially when I mentioned what you said about it being a 'criminal' kinda business. But then all he did was write me another prescription for those same old steroid pills of his. You know, the prednisone. And saying that younger doctors like you had a lot to learn from older men with much more clinical experience."

Another reason to detest Swenson. As if he needed it.

"I see. I want you to know I'll be turning sixty-four in three months time."

"My goodness, that's not young at all. Anyway, getting back to where I was. As soon as I remembered what he said, I started wondering if maybe I broke my hip because you took me off his medicine. Do you think that's at all possible?"

The way this poor lady's thoughts were heading, he could very well find himself in court. But what Adam was to say about her grievously off-the-mark speculation would have little to do with any imperative to protect himself against that unpleasant prospect. His was a different motivation. It was, of course, about staying determinedly candid, but also anticipating, unlike certain previous occasions in which he'd suffered for his candor, that in this instance he might very well stand to see some pleasure from his straightforwardness.

"No, no, that's not even remotely possible. I'm afraid you weren't really listening when you were here in the office. Don't you remember what I said could happen if you kept taking the prednisone?"

"Well you reeled off so many awful possibilities, maybe I kind of lost you there for awhile. I do recall something about ulcers and bleeding, though. But later on, Doctor Swenson said I shouldn't worry about stuff like that. And I was itching so badly when I saw you. It's terribly hard to think about anything else when you've got a rash and that kind of an itch."

It was high time to bite the bullet.

"Mrs. Stevens, I'm very sorry that you didn't fully grasp what I was telling you. But I clearly gave ample and detailed warning that if you didn't come off the prednisone, and do it right away, one of the problems you'd be just about inviting was some kind of a fracture. And you might even, all at once, break not just one, but several bones. Prednisone happens to be a steroid that makes people lose calcium so that their bones begin to soften."

Zelma Stevens was beginning, if a little late, to catch on. And yet she still had questions.

"Oh my God, how could this be? Why? Why? Why?"

Adam didn't have to dig far to answer that one.

"It's been well known for at least forty years."

"Is that why my orthopedic surgeon took me off the prednisone right away? He knew about it, also?"

"That's right. He'd have to. It's common medical knowledge. And your bones are probably still very soft. That's why the pin came loose."

"But Doctor Swenson..."

Time for what could be the coup de grace.

"Swenson? The man's a jackass. A pig-headed, uncaring, ignorant jackass."

"Doctor Merritt, what should I do?"

"Do? There's only one thing to do. It's whatever your orthopedic surgeon tells you to do."

"That's it? That's all?"

"Well if you don't have one, I can recommend a hell of a good lawyer."

He gave her both of Irwin's telephone numbers, the one for his office and the home number.

Immediately on hanging up, he called Irwin, recounting what had been going on. By this time, Irwin had a reasonably good idea of what to expect these days from his friend and client. It was because he did, that he chose not to escalate the demands of such continued representation.

"There's just no stopping you, Adam. Is there? Look, I'm not a medical negligence lawyer. Remember? I just do your tax and real estate work. I only went with you to that medical society fiasco because you were in a jam and needed help in a hurry. Besides which, how would it look if this town's dermatology bad boy and professional nuisance goes and sics his own personal attorney on his archenemy?"

Adam had never been a good listener.

"What I'm thinking is no other lawyer this woman might hire would get the kind of prepping I can bring to the case working all out and full time behind the scene. And why do you have to be a malpractice lawyer to win this one? This case is a slam dunk. That son of a bitch will settle out of court first chance he gets. It'd be too embarrassing for him to go to court and try to defend something as flagrantly wrong as this. It was totally off the wall to leave a woman on prednisone that long for just a simple itch. And remember, the woman's orthopedic surgeon is on record for having stopped it. So you wouldn't even have to get a dermatologist to testify as your expert. But say you did. It'd be real easy. For something this out of line, they'd be coming in here from all over."

Irwin still wasn't buying.

"If she calls me I'll give her the names of some other lawyers. But that's all I'm going to do. And if you insist on getting in over your head, that's entirely up to you. I'm advising against it, but it's your decision and your neck. Me? I'm sticking to what I know something about. And it's not medical malpractice. So go see some patients and I'll be about my own business. Take care, Adam."

The following day Adam got a call from a Ralph Girardi.

"Doctor? My name's Girardi. I'm a lawyer here in town. A Zelma Stevens has been calling my office all day long. She says she's in such deep trouble she can't come down to the office, but that you know all about it. Want to fill me in?"

Girardi got quite an earful.

Nineteen

Odd to feel comfortable that everything was in place and that there was nothing to do but await further developments.

Adam followed his customary routines, examined patients, heard Annie out on everything under the sun, and strove unavailingly to get back into Willy's good graces. It was all done calmly, matter of factly, given the double security of knowing he'd managed to recognize his love for Betty and that Swenson would soon have his comeuppance. He hadn't a single thought for this being a rather odd coupling, or that it had all come about by an extraordinarily quick behavioral shift, much out of keeping with his previous way of being. Nor was he really all that bothered by the loss of his university appointment, at what should have been the peak of his professional career, or having to face up to the serious possibility of a fall off in patient referrals. He accepted all of it, especially since it had not escaped him that by dint of his former, more conventional manner of practicing dermatology, as well as sound investment advice from Ed, he'd come by a pretty good financial nest feathered well enough to withstand most any storm.

Set aside, at least for the time being, was guilt over the radio, or regret that his enigmatic Betty had wound up hating him. All of that dissolved in the sense that finally, and maybe for all time, he had her where there existed no further privilege of escape. She'd never be taking off on him again; there was no further place for her to go. So what if where he'd secluded her, she'd already been cloistered for years? He'd arranged a vital alteration. He'd rendered that place of hers unique. From now on, no one else might find her there, not even Eric. It was theirs alone. And it carried the reassuring stability, the calmness of the grave. Not once did he wonder if he might be slipping.

Fortunately, Annie never gave pause to ask why he spent so much time at night, upstairs in their bedroom, hovering over the radio, nor why so much good music could suddenly be heard coming from it. Until now, it had emitted only the worst kinds of local music plus a lot of static. If she'd quizzed him about it he'd have had to confess that in order to hear Betty's and his kind of music, he'd hauled the radio back to the same repair shop and had it rigged so that discretely and undetected, he could hook it up to a small portable CD player. That was a damned sight better than having to drag the thing back and forth between Richmond and New York.

Although Annie, wondering always what might come next, was ever watching him on the sly, only once did she come close to starting something.

"My, that's a lovely *Boheme*, isn't it?"

"It sure is."

Not appreciating how peculiar he'd become, he had no reason to wonder at the degree of her forbearance.

In no time at all, Zelma Stevens retained Girardi as her lawyer so that during the months following the filing of her complaint against Swenson, Girardi would often phone Adam at night to be better briefed on the medical intricacies of her case. During these rather long talks Adam also conveyed whatever he could regarding Swenson's dealings and personality.

Girardi seemed delighted to learn how overbearing Swenson was and how much he treasured his carefully crafted reputation. At the end of their last discussion, Girardi informed him that some time soon, Mrs. Stevens, who by then had convalesced from a second hip operation, would be required by Swenson's lawyer to give evidence before trial, in the form of a sworn deposition. Adam smiled and went back to his Boheme.

Two weeks later, Girardi called again.

"Well the fat's in the fire. Zelma's been deposed."

"How'd it go?"

"You would've loved it, or maybe your ears were burning. No matter what they asked, all she'd say was what a wonderful doctor you happened to be and what a dumb bastard Swenson was. Only one problem."

"What's that?"

"Well before I could object, they got her to say you were the one who put her on to me."

"But I didn't. It was Irwin."

"Come on, doc. This little lady is all about details. She tracked it from beginning to end. Your calling her. Her calling Irwin. And his recommending me. Then she gave them a damned lecture on all the possible side effects of the prednisone Swenson had her on. I betcha Swenson's lawyer learned more about steroids from Zelma than he ever got from his own doctor. Thought I'd better let you know."

"Never mind. It still sounds good to me."

"Yes. But what about repercussions for you? We didn't count on her spilling the beans. I even warned her about not involving you any, but once she got up to speed there was just no stopping her. That little woman is a dynamo."

"Look. Don't sweat it. In fact I'm beginning to feel even better, now that Swenson figures I masterminded the whole damned thing."

"Okay. Soon as I hear from the other side I'll let you know."

In another three weeks Girardi called to say they'd settled the case. Zelma would get a million dollars.

It didn't take much longer for Adam to receive another letter. This one wasn't hand carried. It came to his office by registered mail and it wasn't from the Richmond medical society. It was quite official looking and out of the offices of the professional licensing board of the commonwealth of Virginia. The board was summoning him to appear. There was no indication what for.

Here was something else for Annie and him to wonder about. She, not knowing everything that had been going on, could only pose what might under other circumstances, be fairly relevant questions.

"How about narcotics? You haven't been over prescribing them, have you?"

"Oh come on, I don't even use them."

"And you've been keeping good office records? Like for lab results and stuff like that? Right?"

When they'd first met, Annie had been a hospital administrator.

"You want me to wait while you review your old accreditation manuals? Look, this has got to be either one helluva something else or a mistake. I'd better get hold of Irwin."

"I don't see that at all. Why does calling Irwin have to be your very first reaction every time you've got some kind of a professional problem? I should think you'd just go on down there and find out what it's all about. Once they spot a lawyer they're bound to believe you've either got something to hide or done what needs expert defending."

"Good God, you're beginning to sound just like that bunch in the medical society."

"You wouldn't like to know exactly what I'm thinking? What a surprise. If I remember correctly, that's your wish, not only for yourself, but for all of us."

"That's not it. I just don't kid myself, anymore. Swenson's got it in for me so badly, I wouldn't put it past him to pull almost anything."

"Well, suit yourself. But there's something I need to say. And I want you to take a moment to think about it. It just so happens that long before you ever got off on your true confession kick, I was always on the level with you. And that hasn't changed any. If my tongue doesn't start wagging over every fool thought that comes my way, it doesn't make me any less ingenuous or sincere than you are. Get my drift? Evidently, you needed to be inspired to it. Ever stop to think there might be people, just ordinary people, who without some kind of a calling or having particularly to work at it, are just what they seem to be and actually say what they think?"

"But not completely. Not everything. So it's not the same. And it's not what counts."

"Mister All-Encompassing Wonderful, that's you. Right?"

"Look, the way I see it, it didn't take long for people to catch on that the only way relationships would work was either to keep your lip buttoned or to con the next guy. Everything proceeded from there. So that nowadays, everybody's wound up living a double life. One's inner, the other's what's out there for public or personal consumption. For some obscure reason, and I have no idea what it might be, I just can't live like that anymore. Call it an internal programming failure, or whatever you like, it seems I've switched back to how we may have started out. What you get is what I think. But not quite totally. There's one exception."

"Yes?"

"It's something I can't tell you about. But I'm working up to it."

"Do me a favor. Don't work too hard."

Glad for the reprieve, he resumed their suspended discussion of the problem at hand.

"Okay. So you want me to pass on Irwin and go by myself. All right, I'll do it. On one condition."

"What would that be?"

"You come along."

"Take Willy."

"Can't. He's not too friendly any more. It's got to be you."

"Forget it."

In any event, what risk was there in showing up without Irwin? After all, the licensing board wasn't like the medical society. He couldn't very well escape any penalties it might mpose by tendering his resignation. Because resigning would mean giving up his license to practice medicine and self inflicting the worst possible penalty. Anyway, having Annie along might be a nice fence mending gesture of sorts, especially if he took her advice and left Irwin out of it.

"Oh come on. Why not?"

Her quick turnabout was unexpected.

"Well what the hell? I'll go."

Twenty

The evening scheduled for his hearing before the licensing board had turned cold and damp. Yet on their drive downtown, Annie was taken by his contrasting high spirits.

"What gives? Just glad to be getting it over with?"

"I suppose. But more like I'm finally getting to have my say."

"Your say? About what? Is this going to be the something you haven't let me in on yet?"

"Not really. I just figure that these guys, even though I don't know a single one of them, are gonna' have at me just like that right wing bunch over in the medical society. So it's high time to let it all hang out, once and for all, and to give them a piece of my mind."

"My God, Adam! You were saying it might all be a big mistake."

"Take my word for it. It's no mistake. There's a master hand behind it. And I'm willing to bet it's Swenson's. But once you're fully prepared to give up everything, it could be kinda fun."

"Pull over and let me out of here. I'll take a cab back to the house."

"You don't mean that. Besides, your being along is apt to take them by surprise and could even give me a strategic advantage. Let's not even announce who you are. You just sit next to me and look like you're taking notes. They'll be wondering are you my secretary or maybe some hot shot lady lawyer."

"What do you mean give up everything?"

"Well here it is in a nutshell. If Swenson's put these guys up to coming after me, what stands to be my real options? It seems to me I can either abide by their ruling or just like last time, try and get beyond their reach. To do that I'd have to throw in the license, quit, retire. But so what? So what if I never look at another dumb skin rash or take off another mole? I've even been thinking lately that if ten years from now I'm still doing what I do now, that'd be ten years down the drain, wasted. Anyway, I'm starting to find that practicing dermatology is a bit of a bore. It really doesn't take much by way of brain power. In fact, you might say that about medicine in general. And the other dividend is that if I surrender the license, I'd have a totally free hand in dealing with Swenson. Which would give me quite a charge."

Annie eyed him stolidly, then turned to stare past the thrashing windshield wipers, as if straining to provide form somehow, to what looked like a shaky future.

"You are just spoiling for a fight, aren't you? That's what this has actually come down to. Hasn't it? Even if this should turn out being some kind of a huge mistake, you're going to start something, anyway. Right? But for what? Just so you can pop off at Swenson? I really don't see it. I don't see it at all. It's like all of a sudden, you've turned paranoid."

Adam had no particular plan of action but he knew there was much more to be done than to merely "pop off at Swenson." At the moment, however, he was neither thinking about what that might be, nor how his wife was taking all of this. Rather, he was imagining a very special witness to his impending encounter with the Virginia licensing board. He had set himself to wondering how Betty would react to his throwing away a hard earned professional career just to get even with a guy like Swenson. She'd be on his side. He'd bet on it.

"Well if not you, I'll bet there are those who'd see it, and see it just fine."

"What's that supposed to mean? I swear you're getting worse and worse. Explain that crack and right now."

"No time. We're there. And for this one, I'm not bein' late."

Adam parked his car in a garage beneath the building occupied by the offices of the licensing board. Riding the elevator up to the top floor, he sensed that Annie was eyeing him intently.

"What's wrong? My tie on crooked or something?"

"No. Just having my last look at Adam, the doctor."

"Don't give it a second thought. It's no big deal. I'm already feeling free of a burden. But you know? Every so often, I do wonder. After all these years of being a doctor, can anyone reasonably hope to see things again without the infernal taint of that kind of a mental warp. I sure hope so. But chances are the business of learning almost anything, not just medicine, messes up your mind so badly, you don't really feel right anymore. The genuine, down-to-earth feelings wind up getting shelved as soon as you get on these learning kicks. So what do you do should the time come that you want to get back to basics? Know what I mean? When you want to re-experience all of those good vibrations, that were once so easy to come by before they got schooled away by stuff that never really took us anywhere, or answered a single important question."

Their elevator had reached the top floor and the automatic door stood open. His wife had questions also.

"We gonna ride this thing up and down all night or do we get off?"

A secretary for the board was seated at her desk a few feet from the elevator. She must have been wondering the same thing.

"You people lost or something?"

Adam emerged from the heady foray with his wife.

"No. That is, unless the verdict's already in, we're not. In point of fact, we are Doctor Merritt and companion."

She might only have been a low level secretary, yet instantly, she had the knowing look of being on to something dark.

"Oh yes. Everybody else is here and waiting. Just follow me and I'll lead you in."

Adam decided to be reassuring.

"Thank you very much. And don't you worry about us one little bit. We're not only fast learners but we're old hands at this kinda' thing. Would you like to hear about our recent meeting with the medical society?"

As they trailed behind her, the young woman mumbled some kind of a quickly garbled declination. And shortly, they found themselves in a small conference room, face to face with four dour looking men and an equally harsh looking woman, all of whom were seated around a long table. Without so much as an introduction, a gray bearded tweedy sort, the apparent leader of the pack, went right to it.

"Please take a seat. We, the governing members of this board, have come upon certain information that we find deeply troubling."

Adam decided on decorum, at least for openers.

"Merritt's my name, Adam Merritt. And this is about me, right?"

The leadoff man took instant umbrage.

"Of course, sir. What else?"

"I dunno. Just checking. People do make all kinds of mistakes. No? We're only human. Right?"

There was no evident willingness to buy that proposition.

"May I continue?"

"Sure. By the way, what's your name? If I might ask."

"Reynolds. Irving Reynolds, in case you plan on suing me also."

There could be no question, now, of what this was all about. But Adam decided to play dumb, anyway.

"I'm not sure I follow you."

"Well you will, sir. Just listen and you most certainly will."

Reynolds might be an even bigger stuffed shirt than anybody Adam had encountered among the members of the medical society.

"I'll be all ears. And I can see that you're the kinda' man who's all heart."

Reynolds pressed on in his bombastic way, pointedly disregarding the innuendo.

"This board has received a declaration that you have

urged a patient under your care to file a malpractice claim against a Doctor Swenson."

"Not true. I merely told that poor woman that what Swenson did was medically unacceptable, and when she seemed at a loss as to how to proceed, I saw to it that she got the names of some lawyers. What she might do about it was entirely up to her. And as far as I'm aware, there's nothing either illegal or unethical about any of it."

Reynolds wasn't buying.

"Moreover, you threatened that unless she took Swenson to court, you'd no longer be her doctor."

Adam wondered, very seriously, if his brain was not surging against the very bounds of its cranial confinement. Or if something in that specific area, wasn't on the very verge of exploding.

"Hey, get real. That's an outrageous lie. Zelma Stevens never got anything like that from me."

Which was all news to Reynolds.

"Who's Zelma Stevens? This is about Alice Peters."

"Who?"

"Alice Peters. Are you telling the members of this board that there are other patients you've been pressuring to sue Doctor Swenson?"

Adam knew he'd made a mistake, a big one. Apparently, these people knew nothing about Zelma and him. But who the devil was Alice Peters?

"Now look here. You all just hold off a bit while I think this through. Because right off the top of my head, I don't remember anyone by that name."

Reynolds decided to have a go with his helpful side.

"Suppose I told you she had recurrent bouts of iritis, osteoporosis, and..."

"And a cancer, an easily operable malignant melanoma that Swenson just took pictures of for more than a year, during which time the damned thing spread all over the place. Okay. Now I remember. But that woman's been dead for two, three years. Maybe even longer."

Reynolds looked deeply gratified.

"Aha, so you do remember, hey? You admit it. Right?"

"What the devil are you talking about? That woman's dead. Dead by courtesy of Swenson's neglect. She's not up to suing anyone, much less saying I tried to pressure her into it."

"That's right. It's her husband. Doctor Swenson's got a sworn statement from Mister Peters, who incidentally thinks the world of Doctor Swenson, that after their first and only visit to your office you were on the phone to them repeatedly, urging them to take Doctor Swenson to court. And saying that if they didn't, you wouldn't give her any further treatment. Fortunately, they decided you were dead wrong and that it was just a matter of their having had a run of bad luck."

Adam liked the idea of fighting fire with fire. And a little invective wouldn't hurt either.

"This is all bullshit, trumped up bullshit. I don't know how Swenson's managed to get old man Peters to say what he's apparently willing to say, but use your head, man. How can you be such a sap? And I don't treat metastatic melanoma. Nor should any dermatologist treat a melanoma once it's gone metastatic. So how could I say I would, if only they'd waylay old Swenson? All I did was refer that lady posthaste to an oncologist for chemotherapy, never intending or planning in any way to see her again. And that's for damned certain. As for letting them know the blame for what happened to her rested at Swenson's door, what's wrong with that? I don't know what kind of medicine you practice, Reynolds, but whatever it is, I can't believe that you or any other kind of doctor would seriously consider that the way to treat a malignant melanoma is to try and embarrass it to death, by taking snapshots of it! That's not your position, is it? And as for Mrs Peters just having had a run of bad luck, in a way that's right. But it had nothing to do with her skin tumor. It had to do with going to see Swenson in the first place. If at the very beginning of this horrible business she'd gone to almost anyone else, she'd probably be alive today."

Reynolds had the steely look of a man not susceptible to reconsidering issues already decided upon.

"Well sir, in situations like this it has been the experience of the board that inevitably the defendant comes up with some kind of an alibi and..."

"Alibi? Are you crazy, man? I'm telling you exactly what happened. And unless you have some way of getting it otherwise from Mrs Peters in her grave, you can't possibly fall for this phony fabrication."

"What you are forgetting, Doctor Merritt, is that against your word we have that of not one, but of two people, who claim quite differently."

"Yeah, oh sure. The word of the husband who's maybe an early Alzheimer, or being pressured somehow, and that of a mean little bastard who's got it in for me, for other reasons."

"These are all unsupported contentions on your part and cannot possibly be grounds for consideration by any of us."

It was then that the single female member of the board decided it was time to get her two cents in.

"Pardon me, but did I hear you admit something about a Zelma Stevens? Words to the effect of her also being pressured to sue Doctor Swenson? Was that what I heard you say?"

Adam had had it.

"Lady, with a closed mind like yours, there's just no telling what's going to get registered upstairs. But in short, very short, you've got it all wrong."

Reynolds looked like they were done.

"Anything else, Doctor Merritt?"

"Well if this kind of crap is what I have to take from here on in as the price for being a licensed doctor, maybe, like in that old stageshow, I'd rather you just call me Mister."

Reynolds jumped at the opening.

"Well sir, that can be easily arranged."

Adam turned to Annie who was sitting next to him, and drawn up rather stiffly. He thought she was looking uncharacteristically militant. Before he could rise to leave, she was on her feet, almost shouting, and shaking a fist at the lone woman of this bunch.

"You, madam doctor, are a senile old prejudiced fool."

Then she let loose in Reynold's direction.

"And you are a nasty minded fossil."

Leaning over Adam's right ear, in a differing hushed tone, she murmured, unmistakably with fondness, exactly what he wanted to hear. "Come on, love. We're gonna beat it."

Twenty-one

It had become eight o'clock and they'd not eaten since lunchtime. Exiting the garage, Annie offered a suggestion.

"How about going for Chinese?"

"Good idea. Maybe Peking duck?"

"You're on. I can taste the plum sauce already."

It was a short drive to the Beijing Palace, during which few words passed between them. And these were mostly confined to bitter characterizations of the members of the licensing board as well as their mutually avowed resolve to escape the risk of foreseeably similar situations in the future. Annie kept repeating herself.

"I had no idea. I simply had no idea. My God, what happens to these people when they get to be doctors?"

"It's like I was saying on the way down. It doesn't take much, by way of schooling, for people to utterly lose touch with reality. And it's not just doctors. It goes with making almost anything of yourself. The question is, how do I work this thing through? Retaliate somehow? Give them all what for? Or do we just stick with what we've been doing? Get beyond their reach. I tell you, though, if

I don't have my licks with Swenson, I think it'll eat me up. I could kill that guy."

"Hey."

"Listen to me, I'm dead serious. I mean it. I can see myself coming up behind him some dark night in the hospital parking lot, and when nobody's looking, I blow him away."

"You're kidding."

"I'm not. And remember, I say what I mean and mean..."

"No more. Please, Adam, no more! It was better, so much better, when you kept things to yourself. Here. Park on the street. The lot's too crowded."

The Beijing Palace was a neighborhood restaurant favored by local families. Even full up it was a comfortable place to eat because the generous size of its two dining rooms permitted a decent separation of tables. Also, the service was first rate. Wine, appetizer, main course, dessert, and tea, were customarily gotten through in no more than ninety minutes, flat.

On this occasion, they'd no real need of a menu because the duck had already been decided upon. So to look it through, after ordering their usual bottle of a decent California Merlot, was for Adam, more habit than need.

But the menu did provide him with a few moments of quiet time, during which he could observe his wife of some twenty-five years. She was searching her own menu, in faint hope of spotting what had always been a rather unlikely find in such a restaurant, a good dessert. Something better than the usual fare of fortune cookies, custard, lichee nuts, or vanilla ice cream. This was a good woman. A damned good woman. The only other one he'd ever eaten Chinese with, had been Betty.

What an odd recollection. One which certainly hadn't surfaced during those days he'd strained for every conceivable remembrance. But there she was.

Once again, he could see her. They were together, seated side by side, in that cheap, rundown place with the cracked and dirty floor tiles over near Third Avenue, a couple of blocks from Bellevue. She had her elbows pressed against the table, a table no doubt long gone too, and was looking perplexed over her inability to select from assorted listings of chicken, lamb, shark fin, pork, shrimp, and so much other standard Chinese fare.

Finally giving up, and twisting around to him for advice, her left knee had all of a sudden bumped or rubbed against his. And it had felt marvelous. If only he'd had the presence of mind to follow through with a countering move of his own knee. Or been bold enough to reach a hand under that table and squeeze her somewhere, anywhere.

But they'd played the game required, their agreed to game, each acting as if there'd never been, nor could ever be, any kind of a genuine physical contact between them.

Annie had said something he'd missed.

"What did you say?"

"I asked if you're still up for the Peking duck? It's for two, you know."

"Sure, sure. But there's something important that I've got to get off my chest."

"Now? For God's sake, Adam. Right now?"

"It's not for His sake. It's for mine. I think I've developed feelings for someone."

"What?"

"Take it easy, it's not what you think. It's the one from

Bellevue who died. Anyway she's dead, and there was never anything between us."

Annie grabbed her menu and waved it before his face. "You look here. I've been searching everywhere on this fool thing for a decent piece of cake. But let me tell you something. When it comes to cake, you really take it. As for me, this could just about clinch it once and for all. What are you trying to tell me? That our marriage was and is a sham? A mistake? Some kind of a big joke? That my life's been wasted? That I should have hooked up with someone else, maybe even someone who wanted kids and done better for myself? That it was another woman you really wanted? Is that what I'm to understand? Or is it that you've finally gone stark raving mad?"

"Now look..."

"No, you look. What I'm thinking, what any reasonable person would hope to be thinking, that's if after something like this they still had their wits about them, is that you've got problems now, real, big-time problems that need sorting out. I'll give you that. But if instead of making the right adjustments, you're gonna see if you can't avoid them by drifting off into some kind of a fantasy world, well you go right to it, but on your bloody own. I'll be cutting out. Because anyone with the least hold on their senses would tell you this is no time to be dredging up and going cuckoo over some big time, ancient, adolescent infatuation. What'd you do last night? Have one of your weird dreams? Is that what started this off? Don't you think we all have crazy reminiscent stuff like that? But what the rest of us do is we wake up, we come to our senses, and we shake them off. Adam, I don't know whether to smash you or break down and cry."

She did look rather ready for tears.

"It's not because of a bad dream. It's nothing that simple. It's for real."

A waiter was standing there, patiently waiting for their order. Annie turned his way rather brusquely.

"Bring us the shark fin soup with mushrooms and the Peking Duck with orange sauce and also the plum sauce. We'll have them both. And that's for two, please."

Then she started up again.

"Real, you say. Real. Right? How would you know from real? You've lost all sense of what that might be. So this is the big, big deal you've been holding back on. Right? My God, I can't believe I'm still sitting here with you. That I've even ordered things for us to eat together when I should be splitting, looking for a cab, and maybe also, a lawyer to call my very own."

"I just knew this would happen once I clued you in. I was afraid you'd take it poorly. But now I feel much better. Finally, you've got the whole picture. That's except for some of the details. Like the radio. And Proust. And what I really did up there in New York."

"Let me guess, you bastard. You went to pay your respects at the dear girl's grave? I'll bet it's somewhere out on Long Island. Bring her flowers, did you?"

"I don't really know what they did with her remains. I've absolutely no idea. I'm not even sure they were brought back to the States. You see, she lived and died over in Europe. And her husband was so pissed off at me for ringing him up, he slammed the phone down before I could get all the details. Can I tell you the rest of it? It'd help a lot."

"Help? You? Not on your life. There'll be no more of that. And thanks to you, my appetite's just about demolished.

Damn it, here comes the soup. You take it, take all of it. And for all I care, you can choke on it. I'm sticking with the wine. God knows, I need it now. And don't so much as think about uttering another word. You just sit there and go back to figuring how you're gonna deal with the licensing board, or how to best knock off Swenson. I'll try and forget you're even here, and start praying that, somehow, I get to feel like eating again. And no way, no way ever, do you get my sympathy about anything. From here on in, you made your bed? Well mister, you lie in it."

"Oh come on, Annie... It's all in the past."

"Don't you start nudging me. I'm gonna drink. Maybe later, I'll force myself to eat a little something."

When the duck did finally make its entry upon this charged up scene, she actually did quite well by it. So did he. In fact, Adam just about matched her bite for bite. That was because, while her appetite had suffered, his had been invigorated, so relieved was he that now, finally, he could consider himself a fully self revealed and honest person.

Also, he had the feeling now, that in a way, Betty was even more on board with regard to his conflicts with Swenson and the Virginia Licensing Board. Before this, she'd seemed to merely give the nod to how he was handling it. Although maybe once or twice, kind of egging him on. But now he had the distinct notion that Betty might be taking a fresh look at the entire situation, and as a matter of fact, wasn't liking it much that he'd ever thought, either back then or now, of grabbing for her under the table.

Right up and through the serving of the duck, the only looks he'd gotten from Annie were clear warnings of a dangerously aggravated disapproval of his escalating and bizarre waywardness.

But if she wouldn't respect his need to talk some more, maybe he could try something else. The something he'd not dared with Betty. He took her by surprise while she was busy attempting, as adeptly as possible, to top off her last Peking duck pancake with a mound of scallions and plum sauce.

"What the hell's gotten into you now?"

"I can't even give you a squeeze?"

"Here? There? Under the table?"

"It's illegal?"

"No, just dumb and childish. And considering everything, not in the least bit welcome."

"Look. Just because I'm kind of partial to the memory of this old gal doesn't mean I've stopped going for you big time. In fact, right now, I'm feeling I could love you to death. How about later? Could we fool around a little?"

"I'll think about it, once I've had the ice cream and lichee nuts."

"Terrific. And I get to tell the rest of my story?"

"I suppose. After all, that's bound to be better than leaving it to my imagination. Because Adam, these days, I wouldn't put anything past you."

Driving home, and during a late night reaffirmation of what they still had together, Adam had two thoughts. First, that Annie and he were probably in it for the long run. Surely there was that. But also, and no doubt about it, either. Betty had grown downright enthusiastic for the way things had been going. Which was a real puzzle.

Twenty-two

His medical license was suspended for three months, starting in thirty days. Notice of the board's action came in the following week's mail. There'd be twenty-one days for an appeal.

Having gotten the word that morning, Annie took the latest bad news in stride.

"Well? You've always wanted to take one of those 'round the world Cunard cruises."

"With you seasick half the time? Forget it."

"So go by yourself. I'll stay home with Willy and look after things. Who knows? Maybe some starry night, when you're up on deck, that old Betty of yours might just materialize."

"Very funny. I'll tell you one thing though. I'm sure not looking to appeal. Not to that bunch. I know it'd get me nowhere. And besides, I don't fancy getting down on my knees to those bastards. But I might take them to court. Sue for cause, loss of income, maybe even punitive damages. I'll talk to Irwin."

Annie shook her head vigorously.

"And be in a stew for years, waiting for your day? Then maybe losing, anyway, and getting stuck for costs? Not only yours, but theirs as well? I shouldn't think so."

"Well it's either take 'em on, somehow, or throw in the license entirely. No way do I go sneaking off with my tail between my legs."

"Who's to know anything about it? It'd be like an extended vacation or a kind of sabbatical. Doctors are always doing things like that. You could even sign up for one of those world health trips. You know, those hospital ships that go off to the far east and third world places."

"Look. Everybody's gonna know. The board will surely publicize it as a reprimand with punitive action, and Swenson will not only be gloating, he'll be talking it up."

"Not necessarily."

"Okay. Have it your way. Not necessarily, but probably enough for me to bank on it. Besides, I've got this feeling that what I really need, is to get a helluva lot madder about the whole damned situation."

"What earthly purpose would that serve?"

"You hit it on the head. A real down to earth one. If all I do is see if I can't connive my way out of this, or simply go and surrender the license, or even if I drag everybody into court, none of that's the genuine article. It's slow, and tedious, or by the book, but worse, it's no substitute for reacting naturally and blowing my stack. You know, come on full blast and not sidestep it. I need to let off some steam. That may not get me anywhere in practical terms, but at least I'd have it off my chest. Anything short of going berserk is not gonna fill the bill."

"I can't believe I'm hearing this."

"Believe it. If I don't come on strong about something like this, it'll eat me up. That's how you get an ulcer or a coronary and probably half the skin rashes that wind up in my office."

Annie decided on a quick recap.

"So to save your mind, and body too, you're looking to become a raving maniac. No? Get even worse than you are already. Well, okay. You go right to it. But at least tell me this. How much time do I have for splitting before you go into your Mister Hyde routine?"

Adam had no ready answer. He fidgeted, looking pained, although they were in the den and he had settled into his most comfortable chair.

Getting no answer, Annie continued.

"I should head on out, right away?"

"Cool it. You've got all the time in the world."

"Thank God."

"The problem is, say what I may, and although it's easy enough for me to call every last one of them a bastard, they don't really rile me that much. At least, I don't stay terribly stirred up. Maybe I've spent so many years dealing with these pompous asses, I've become indifferent to it. It seems that once I've had my initial reaction, I'm not inclined to fly off the handle like I used to, even when they've turned on me for no good reason. So what I'm saying is that I find all this more annoying than grounds to go bonkers. And that's a pity because I need to get mad. Really big time mad. Or I can just see myself slipping into one helluva funk. Know what I mean?"

"No. We ladies place a high premium on practicality and level headedness."

"Anyway, I'm gonna give Irwin a ring. And who knows?

Maybe one of these guys will cross the line and set me off. Be my bloody salvation."

Without further words, his wife got up to leave.

"Hey, where you goin'?"

"Shopping. Don't wait up."

"What do you mean don't wait up? It's not even noon."

"I need a break from all this. They've just opened an all-night supermarket at the mall. I could stay over."

"Big joke. See you later? Around two o'clock?"

"Oh sure. After all, I need to see how all of this is going to end."

"By two o'clock?"

"Exactly. I'm hoping that Irwin will talk some sense into you. Bye bye."

No chance of that. At least not right then. When Adam called Irwin's office, the word he got was that Irwin had gone out of town on depositions and wouldn't be back for three days.

Unfortunately, it was Wednesday. On Wednesdays Adam saw no patients. It was his day off, and the office was closed. Which meant there'd be no diversion. He considered heading over there, anyway, and starting on whatever might be needed during the three month period of suspension. No point to it. Should he decide to give up his license, he'd be closing the place down for good.

Then he thought of a different office, Swenson's, over at the university. That mean old son of a bitch didn't take Wednesdays off. Adam could just about see him there, self-satisfied, smug, and no doubt smirking, while he went about his business, pleased to know he'd won out with his well engineered retaliation for having been forced to settle up with Mrs. Stevens.

Might that not be the better place to head? Turning up there, if only to pop in briefly, would be sure to infuriate his nemesis. And even though his services were no longer wanted or welcome at the university, he still did have his academic appointment as professor. He had every right to stop by, pick up mail, browse, schmooze some with the department secretaries, and offer up whatever comments or advisements his new status, whatever that might be, called for. The more he thought about such an excursion, the more he considered it a sound idea. So taking the car, off he went. He was bent, for the most part, on coming face to face with Swenson.

As soon as he set foot in the dermatology office the staff seemed to freeze, but then became ever so busy. All eyes stayed rigorously averted, but extra senses appeared to have let everyone in on his brazenly unheralded appearance. The attention of all three secretaries, as well as that of the departmental administrative assistant, was uncustomarily directed at computer screens, as all four of them almost frantically trolled through records and schematics he'd never seen booted up before. And when he said "hello," the administrative assistant turned his way, but looked not a little nonplussed.

"Doctor Merritt?"

"The one and only?"

"What can we do for you?"

"Nothing much. Just picking up my mail."

"You don't have any."

"That's reassuring."

"I'm not following you."

"Well these days there's no telling what your boss in here," Adam said, thumbing in the direction of Swenson's door, "might be hatching up for me and dropping in the mail."

"Please Doctor Merritt, as I've told you once before, that kinda' stuff is way out of my league."

Adam's next idea could have been somehow prompted. Because its awfully quick vocal expression came as much of a surprise to him as to the dumbfounded administrative assistant who heard it.

"Give him a buzz. Tell him I'm here."

"I think he knows. His door is shut. And usually it's open. Even when there's someone with him."

Adam insisted.

"Buzz him anyway."

"I'd better not. He wouldn't like it."

"Buzz him."

"I can't. I won't."

"Okay. Is his door locked?"

"It's never locked. There's never been a key to it."

Adam stepped past the assistant's desk and ever so slowly, pushed against Swenson's door. He was immediately challenged. His gnome-like enemy, now cornered and irate, was visibly shaken by this surprise intrusion. He sprang from his chair.

"What are you doing here, Merritt? You know you've no place here."

"How come? I'm not a professor in this department?"

"Not for very long, you are. That's something we intend to see about next."

Adam acted as if he'd not heard Swenson's threat, even turning a bit conciliatory.

"You wanna know something? I'm truly baffled by most of this. All I ever did was tell two of your patients that you'd screwed up. Screwed up rather badly. Now you had to have known you'd screwed up. So big deal. Not only did you and I know it, but the patients were of the same understanding. What the hell's so terrible about that? Wasn't it right for them to know? And when Mrs. Stevens decided to do something about it, wasn't that right also?"

"Don't you dare speak to me about right or wrong. You are in no position to. You couldn't possibly be the one to preach to me."

"Why not? Isn't that what this whole thing comes down to?"

"We are not in church."

"Do we have to be?"

"And you are not my God."

"You've got one?"

"Of course."

"Which one? I'm starting to wonder."

"You get out of here, Merritt, before I call security."

Adam stared at his chairman. The little man was in a frenzy. He'd gotten red faced. His head was jerking side to side, and an outstretched right hand, increasingly tremulous, was pointed dead at him.

"Oh come on, Swenson. Simmer down. Why can't you and I talk it over and have us an absolutely honest take on all of this?"

Swenson went from lobster red to dark livid. He caught his breath then screamed that same command.

"Get out, get out. I'll see you in hell, I will."

The malediction, along with the sputtering little man's quite demoniacal features, gave Adam what seemed like a quick glimpse of exactly what he was up against.

"So that's the deal, is it? And you'd like a quick taste of what's on the final agenda, hey?"

Adam lunged for Swenson. Soon he was hearing a rasping or croaking sound as fingers (were they really his?) closed around the vile little man's neck. He thought, also, that he could hear something crack down where Swenson's larynx was located as his hands became locked in an unrelenting, harsh spasm of contraction.

His hateful foe was collapsing under him, but Adam was also going down, as they sprawled across the top of Swenson's desk.

He had a disturbing thought. It was about Annie and Willy having to cope with his being put away, possibly for good.

But much worse was a vision of his Betty, looking pleased as Punch at the sight of him at Swenson's throat.

That was enough to scare the hell out of him.

Twenty-three

But Adam never went to jail. Because on that day in February when this story first began, he was instead startled awake by something he could neither define nor recall.

Nevertheless, he quickly readied for work, and as usual these days, was annoyed for having deferred for so long the major renovation, including a paint job, that his bedroom sorely required. He could hear music coming from the timer rigged, venerable radio left him in trust what seemed a century ago by forthright old Betty. And Willy, of course, was also there to get him up by the insistent authority of a very cold and moist Doberman nose.

Heading for the bathroom, he chanced to wonder once more, as so often he'd done over the last few years, what had ever become of Betty. Surely, it was now more than twenty years since her last letter from Holland. Or was it from Switzerland?

No matter. Not important. Even if for all that time she'd never been completely out of mind, this was certainly not the moment to stop and think about it, or he'd be late for work.

And yet, while shaving, he couldn't help but think of her. It was almost as if whatever had been between them, always so elusive, was somehow rekindled overnight and bearing reconsideration.

That drift of thought, and the buzz of his electric razor, were challenged by the persistent ringing of his phone.

"Hello?"

"That you, Doctor Merritt?"

It was a somewhat familiar woman's voice but he couldn't quite place it.

"It's Zelma Stevens, doctor. I'm awfully sorry to bother you at home but I really need to talk to you. If you remember, I saw you when Doctor Swenson was out of town."

"Sure. I remember you. What's the problem?"

"Well, when I saw you last month, if you recall, I was getting all bent out of shape, stooped over like. And what you said was that this sometimes happens with older women when they get past the menopause, but that I should stop taking the prednisone and report back to Doctor Swenson as soon as he was back in town. My x-rays showed what you called an osteoporosis of the spine."

"That's right."

"Well, I did just what you told me. But Doctor Swenson, when he got back, said it'd be okay for me to start on the prednisone again, only to just take one a day instead of two. And then what happened was that I got really bent over and started to have these terrible cramps in my back and my legs, and also a hard time passing my urine."

"I see."

Adam saw it very well. He could even visualize a new set of x-rays showing a compression fracture of the poor woman's spine. Her clinical situation, by history alone, was that straightforward.

But she had a lot more to say.

"Well when that happened I got very frightened and went to see this orthopedic doctor who x-rayed my spine once more, stopped the prednisone just like you did, and right away put me in a body brace. He says that now I've got myself a fracture there. So what I'd like to do, if it's okay with you, is show you the x-rays and see if you agree with how I'm being treated."

"But what about Doctor Swenson?"

"It doesn't seem that I can get to see him until a week from now. His office nurse says he's all booked up until then, and that as far as she's concerned this problem isn't really the kind of situation he'd be treating anyway. She won't put me through to him, and it looks like his home telephone number must be unregistered. At least I can't find it, like I found yours, in the phone book. So can I come and see you?"

"Absolutely. You go right to my office and bring your x-rays with you. Just tell my nurse you spoke to me and that I'm putting you in as my first patient."

"Bless you, doctor."

Returning to his shave, Adam was now being stared back at by a half-stubbled, but fully anxious self. If the truth were known, he'd been worrying about this lady ever since he'd first examined her. And later on, when Swenson was back in town, he'd called him right away to apprise him of what was going on with his patient.

Adam was quite certain that they'd agreed on the relatively urgent need for her to stop taking the prednisone. She'd been on it much too long, and as he recalled,

Swenson was exceedingly grateful that he'd interceded without, in so many words, letting on to Mrs Stevens of the probable tie in between the prednisone and her spine problem. As a matter of fact, Swenson had admitted it was a terrible oversight on his part not to have stopped the drug a lot earlier.

So why the hell had he started it up again, if even at a lower dose? Here was Adam, working a kind of cover up for Swenson, all the while fearful the lady might get worse in spite of being off the prednisone, and meanwhile Swenson was busy compromising everything, maybe even getting the two of them in trouble up to their necks, by giving her still more of the stuff. On top of that, this Zelma Stevens just had to be searching for answers, ones that were a lot better than those she'd gotten so far. So now, what has Swenson's dumb office nurse up and done? She's made it look like Swenson's maybe ducking her. What a deal this could turn into.

Adam didn't bother with much of a breakfast. All he had was a cup of coffee and that on the run. Willy, accustomed to scraps from the breakfast table, looked taken aback by his master's quick and harried departure.

When he arrived at the office, Mrs Stevens was already in the waiting room with an x-ray folder resting across her lap. He had a feeling that with it, she'd come armed well enough to nail both him and Swenson. There was something else to be seen, a not inconsiderable bit of medical paraphernalia she'd neglected to mention. Not only was Mrs Stevens engulfed by a large and cumbersome brace which she'd tried to conceal by draping herself in an oversized white woolen cape, but when Adam motioned her to precede him towards an examining room, she paused and beckoned to his nurse to fetch a big aluminum walker upon which she was now completely dependent for ambulation.

Great, this was just great. What could the other three patients who were sitting there be thinking? After all, his office was a place for rashes and other dermatological trivia. Not hobbled people struggling to make the best of a disastrous complication resulting from negligent treatment. The kind of catastrophic medical misfortune referred to by most doctors, ever so diplomatically, as an "iatrogenic" problem.

It took the unhappy lady almost five minutes to make her awkward way into an examining room. While she was attempting to reach it, Adam studied the x-ray films of her thoracic and lumbar spine. Arrived finally, she promptly collapsed into a chair. He was sympathetic.

"I'm so very sorry to see what's been going on."

"'Going on'? Is it still going on, doctor? I was hoping that whatever it is, it's been stopped."

"Well that's probably so. At least with the brace there's a good chance the spine will heal and remodel itself into something more normal. We would hope that there won't be permanent pressure on your spinal cord."

"And that's what I have? Pressure on my spinal cord?"

Adam was relieved to realize that so far Mrs Stevens was kind of in the dark as to what was actually happening to her. Which left him an opening, as her apparent sole adviser, to head off what could certainly become an ugly situation, not only for Swenson but maybe for him as well.

"Well yes. The last thoracic vertebra has collapsed a little and slipped backwards somewhat so that it just about touches the spinal cord. You know, of course, that I'm no expert on things like this. I'm only a dermatologist. But isn't that what your orthopedic surgeon has told you?"

"Kind of, I guess. But you know how it is when doctors look at you kind of fishy like and don't really say very much. That's why I came to see you. I want to get it all straight in my mind. Last time, as soon as you looked at my x-rays, right away you said `curvature' and `osteoporosis' and `no more prednisone'. And that's what my orthopedic doctor said also. The prednisone is what's done it to me. Isn't that right, Doctor Merritt?"

It was like being called to the witness stand. Fortunately, he'd not been sworn here, to tell the truth, nothing but, and the miserable whole of it. He could hedge a little. Maybe quite a lot.

"I wouldn't put it like that. Women who've never had any steroids, like the prednisone, quite commonly run into this very same situation when they start losing bone calcium after the menopause."

"But right away you said to `cut it' and so did my orthopedic surgeon. It was only Doctor Swenson who said I should start it up again. So what's a person to really believe?"

"Well now. You know that your skin problem has caused you a great deal of grief for just years and years. And no one wanted you to suffer, as long as the prednisone seemed to be working so well for you. Especially Doctor Swenson."

"My God, Doctor Merritt, this is so much worse than that old itch of mine. I've become a cripple!"

"I'm sure, I'm sure. But what I was trying to say is this: The reason for stopping the prednisone was not because anyone had the idea it was at the root of your spine problem. It was only on the uncertain chance that it might make things a little worse for you, or slow down your recovery."

"Really?"

"Quite so."

"That's a relief, doctor."

"There's no good reason for you to have such a concern."

Adam mused, waxing poetically bizarre. Could he count the ways and the times he'd now lied to this sad lady? There were at least three. Possibly more. And all those other times, with other patients? Then it would add up to a great deal more. It was certainly much too many to permit a reliable tally.

"So what am I to do?"

"You mean about your eczema?"

"No. That seems to have gone away."

Adam chose to have her look a little on the bright side. It was a hastily taken strategy.

"There now. Doctor Swenson's banished that quite neatly, hasn't he?"

"I suppose. But I'm talking about my fracture and my spinal cord being out of whack."

"Well the only thing to do about that, is to hang in there with your orthopedic surgeon, and do exactly what he tells you. It seems to me, he's right on top of the situation. Just give it a little more time and I have the feeling it won't be long before you turn the corner quite handily."

"You really think so, doctor?"

"I wouldn't mislead you."

"All right. I feel a little better."

"And take the first appointment you can get with Doctor Swenson. I'm sure he'd want to see you. That thing with his office nurse was probably a simple misunderstanding. Anyway, I'll call him and let him know what's been going on."

"Thank you, doctor. You're very kind."

"Not at all."

Adam rang for his nurse to call a cab and to help Mrs Stevens out.

No sooner than the door had closed behind her, but Adam ducked into his private office to call Swenson. Some officious sounding nurse who answered, tried giving him much the same runaround as had been experienced by Zelma Stevens.

"The doctor's real tied up now. If you want, I can take your number, and maybe when he gets a chance, he'll get back to you."

"Hey, I haven't got time for this. You buzz him and tell him it's me, and that it's an emergency."

"Oh come on now, doctor."

"No, you come on. And if you don't put me through real quick like, there's gonna be hell to pay. You like your job, don't you?"

In no time at all, Swenson was on.

"Adam, my dear friend, what can I do for you? Miss Harris says you're in some kind of trouble?"

What a switch. Or on the other hand, by association with Swenson, that might prove to be just about right.

"Not me. Not either one of us, I'm hoping. That is unless a certain patient of yours wises up to what's been going on."

"Is this some kind of a riddle, Adam? I really haven't got time for one. My office is jam packed and I'm running way behind."

"Your patient Zelma Stevens. That Miss Harris of yours refused to give her an appointment, so she headed over here to see me."

"Well that's all right, Adam. I'm sure you'll do your very best for her. She can see you any time she pleases. Have you thought up something different for her? I've just been carrying her on prednisone, you know."

Oh Adam knew all right. The problem was nobody else had better. Like some cagey lawyer. Or some other doctor. And God forbid, one of those hired gun doctors, the ones who liked to testify as experts in malpractice cases.

"You'd better take some time to listen, because now she's collapsed her thoracic spine, has cord compression, and is barely getting around in a walker. I thought you and I were agreed to keep her off the prednisone when she started to decalcify and developed those first signs of a curvature."

"Adam, when you've been at this game for as long as I have, you get to where you've sort of a nose for it. And that's when you start sorting out fact from fiction. I've never quite bought that business about prednisone, or other steroids, bringing on pathological fractures. It seems to me that past a certain age, it's more a matter of coincidence than any real causal relationship. And besides that, what would you have me do? We can't simply ignore our responsibility to treat her skin condition. Can we? That's what she came to us for in the first place."

Adam didn't want to pull Swenson up too abruptly. After all, the guy was chairman of his department.

"How about just switching over, at least for a while, to topical steroids? That would avoid the systemic side effects."

Swenson shot down, rather curtly, any idea of that being a viable option.

"For my money, they never work. Anyway, what'd you tell her?"

"What I said was that stopping the prednisone, something that both her orthopod and I had both done, was just precautionary on our part, and recommended on no more than the slightest chance that the prednisone was making things worse or slowing down her healing."

"Splendid. Well, that should just about be the end of it."

"'Just about' is what concerns me. Don't forget that this lady came to me today only because she suspected it was the prednisone which was doing her in."

"Well now, Adam. You know how I feel about that. And once you think about it a little longer, I'm confident you'll begin to see it exactly as I do. I've always considered you to be a very smart boy, and I don't expect you're going to disappoint me."

"Thanks."

"No, Adam. Don't thank me. Because I'm the one to be obliged. Obliged for the sound way you're handling this. And when I have the chance, I'll not be forgetting it."

"Remember. She'll be coming to see you."

"No problem. And never fear. From here on in I'll take care of everything."

Adam didn't like the sound of that. It was certainly a mixed bag. Swenson, albeit the most influential dermatologist in town, and however grateful he might be to him, was in the habit of being much too overbearing and sure of himself, for either of their good.

Twenty-four

A rriving home that evening, he was greeted with a question. "You getting forgetful or something? Or did you and Harold have too much to drink last night?"

"Why's that? I did something wrong?"

"You left your radio on."

"Is that all? What happened is I had to take off in a hurry. One of my patients called and needed to be seen before the rest."

"Something serious?"

"Since when do I handle what's serious? I'm your corner skin doctor, remember?"

"How could I forget? Just to look at you is to start itching all over. You sure you don't bring that stuff home with you?"

"Look, if you're all that worried about it, I'll set up a chemical shower right outside the front door and use it before I even come in the place. How would that be?"

"Forget it. You know I'm only kidding."

So was he. But as cover for still another one of his lies. They sure came easily. But why this one? What would be the problem with telling her all about Zelma Stevens? None whatsoever, as far as he could see. But it would need to be such a lengthy account, and he'd just as soon spare himself from even starting on it.

Besides, lying was so easy, ever since, a long, long time ago, he'd gotten the full hang of it. So why, all of a sudden, should he start being different? Different from himself and everybody else. When you came right down to it, lying was how everyone had been doing business, for just about forever.

"So did you turn it off?"

"What?"

"What? The radio."

"Not a chance. Far be it from me to mess around with that contraption. The way you've got it hooked up to that weird looking electronic timer of yours, it's way beyond my simple skills."

"You mean it's still running?"

"You've got me. Last I heard it sounding off was around one o'clock when I came home from the store."

"Christ, it could've burned out."

"The radio?"

"No, the timer. I'd better go look and see."

As Adam headed for the stairs, Annie yelled after him.

"Too bad if it's only the timer that's gone kaput. That damned old radio has gotten to sound just awful. It's become more like a squawk box than anything else. It beats me why you've hung on to it for so long."

From up above, though still on the run, he called down his justification. Another lie.

"Hey, it's from my Bellevue days. That's when I bought it."

Now in the bedroom, he could barely hear her retort.

"Big deal. When are you going to get over that old dump? It always looked to me like it was about ready for tearing down."

Satisfied to find everything upstairs in order, his vintage set still alive and struggling valiantly to do justice to what transmissions it could still pick up, he shouted his reassurance. "It's okay; I've turned it off. It'll probably outlast us both."

"Not on your life, it will. You pass first and the damned thing's going out the back door with you."

Betty would probably like that. After all, she'd made him the radio's permanent custodian.

Why think something so off the mark? Was he not remembering that in her final letter she'd fairly begged, a second time, that he ship it to her? And wasn't he being unmindful, also, of his unforgivable reply? That untruthful letter insisting he'd already sent it, adding that maybe it had been lost in transit?

Adam stared at the radio. Next, he bent over it for a better look, wanting to refresh his memory regarding manufacture. On the right side of its brown bakelite console he could make out a small embedded plaque bearing the brand name. It was a Lafayette model. Lafayette was long out of business and had disappeared from the high fidelity chain store scene. Which was appropriate, because Betty, his old Bellevue flame, had followed and was long gone also.

His old flame? What a peculiar thought! Were it the case, surely one with no heat to it, sputtering from the outset, and promptly extinguished by her determination to love that other guy, the one from Switzerland, the one she called Eric.

Many times he'd wondered of late, in fact, just like this very morning, what had ever happened to the two of them. But having no current mailing address or other leads, there was no way to check it out. Nothing but the vague recollection of her having said she'd grown up in a small California town called Sierra Madre. Like in that old Bogart movie.

Well wasn't this a funny business? It was like one of those deja vu things. The almost sure feeling he'd already phoned somebody out there in California and learned all about her. But learned what? Learned nothing, dammit. Absolutely nothing. Because he couldn't remember anything else, and was dead certain he'd never had either the gumption or so much as a real temptation to do anything of the sort. But strangely sprung or not, it was sure a neat idea.

Neat enough to bug him so badly he couldn't stop thinking about it. Until, no more than a few minutes later, he found himself actually doing it. Connecting with the California operator and then the first of several numbers listed under the name of Tarrington. It happened so fast! And came out of nowhere.

There was a man's voice at the other end.

"You're looking for a Betty Tarrington? A Doctor Betty Tarrington?"

Adam could swear the man was joking around. But the voice continued.

"Well we've got only one of those. Hold on while I get her."

There was a thump. He'd damned well skipped a beat. Now he was skipping a bunch of them. Then he heard a familiar sounding voice. A familiar, somewhat stern voice. And all business-like. Or was it just sounding that way because of the distance?

"Hello. This is Doctor Tarrington. Who's this?"

He was getting the feeling that distance had nothing to do with it. This voice was not in the best of moods.

"It's Adam, Betty. And if I sound like I'm choking it's because I sure am."

"Adam? Adam who?"

"Merritt. Adam Merritt, from Bellevue. You don't remember?"

"Wait a minute. You just wait a minute, while I think."

It wasn't a full minute but the pause was uncomfortably long enough. And sufficient for him to wonder if she was merely kidding him.

"You're the one who took my radio. Right?"

"Took it?"

"Right, took it, you creep. You don't think I bought that baloney about it getting lost, do you? Especially since you never bothered to send me any kind of a receipt I could follow up on."

"I shipped it to you!"

"Lying won't make it so. Well, what do you want?"

Time to change the subject. But what other one could there be, given this kind of a start? A nasty standoff over that miserable radio.

"Well I never imagined I'd find you back in California. At best, I was hoping for an overseas address so I could get in contact, and check on how you all were doing."

"So contact. And as far as I can see, the rest is none of your business."

"Come on, Betty. What about your career and Eric?"

She relented, maybe softening a little.

"Okay. Lets get this over with real fast. Eric and I have been divorced for eighteen years. So I came back here and set up a small town practice in internal medicine. That's it. Period. Off and over."

"Hey, wait up."

"Jesus Christ, what is it now?"

"Just, how are you?"

"Running on borrowed time, you degenerate liar. Last year they had to take off my right breast and now there's been a recurrence of tumor in some of my lymph nodes."

"Oh God, that's terrible."

"God? Leave Him out of it. He's just death and all its nasty implications. That's who He is. Now look here. With time running out for me, I really don't see why I should waste any that might be left, talking to you. Especially since every time I happen to think about what you did with my old radio, it really gets to me. So a pox on you Adam. Goodbye and good riddance."

"Hold it!"

"All right. You want the truth? Think a person like you can handle it?"

"Sure."

"When I first picked up, I was putting you on about having trouble remembering. Right off, I recognized your voice and knew it was you. I've thought about you a lot, even yesterday."

"Really?"

"Right. I happened to be playing *La Boheme*. It was that same recording we had in the old days. And you know where Mimi dies at the end of the last scene, with the curtain falling, and Rodolfo left screaming her name?"

"Of course. How could I ever forget? It was like our very own special music."

"Well I was thinking that I was Mimi and you were

Rodolfo, but with a twist. Because it would be just right and so much better, if when she took off, you got dragged along for wherever she was heading. Now don't bother me any more, you creep."

She'd hung up on him.

Then a voice from below and a disconnected reality, he was so out of sorts.

"Hey, if you're finally off the phone, come on down for supper. I'm not waiting all night to get started, you know."

Twenty-five

It didn't take long for Zelma Stevens to catch on. It might have been some ill-considered remark that Swenson came across with when she had her next and final appointment with him. Or her orthopedic surgeon could have slipped up and tipped her off. However she got the word, in short order it was handily reinforced by the opinions of a medical expert retained by her freshly hired lawyer, to testify on her behalf against Doctor Swenson.

When Swenson called to say he'd been subpoenaed, Adam hoped to stay out of it. After all, why should he be implicated? He'd only acted in good faith, been sympathetic to her situation, satisfied her medical needs when turned to, and was, as a matter of fact, the first doctor to intervene in her interest by stopping the prednisone. The problem was that Mrs Stevens' lawyer apparently considered him the best witness to Swenson's foul up. So Adam got served with a subpoena also.

He'd been named, to his partial relief, not as a defendant but as one of Mrs. Stevens' treating doctors. Unfortunately, it was beginning to look as though whatever incriminating words might be needed to nail old Swenson, were expected to be from out his not too eager mouth.

No sooner than he had his subpoena, Adam was on to Swenson. As usual, he had barely any time to talk. What initial words he had for Adam were more an expression of concern for how Adam was taking all of this, than for any anxious thoughts he himself might have, regarding what, by all rights, should have been an iron clad case against him.

"Now Adam, don't you lose a bit of sleep over any of this. Once you've been dragged through as many of these things as I have, you'll come to realize they're not worth being taken seriously."

Adam hadn't even been sued once.

"I just don't like the idea of being cast as Mrs Stevens' ipso facto, undeclared expert. It looks like they're setting to use me kind of indirectly."

"I'm sure that's not going to happen. My lawyer believes that once you start explaining everything, they'll decide not to even call you."

"What do you mean explain?"

"Well before we ever get to court her lawyer is sure to take your deposition. He has to know exactly what you intend to say once you're on the witness stand. And when he does, that'll be the end of it. It'd be downright foolish for him to call you."

"Good. I didn't fancy being dragged in through the back door and used in any way that might jeopardize your position."

That's when Swenson really unloaded on him.

"Then what we do is we take him by surprise by calling you to the stand ourselves."

"What?"

For a while, Adam had thought he could see clear sailing. Now it was looking more like a shipwreck.

"Sure. That's when you tell them how esteemed I am in dermatology, even all around the world, much less here in Virginia. And how this whole thing, for lack of any merit at all, is nothing but a storm in a teapot."

To Adam, it was still looking like a damned shipwreck, and he a castaway with no place to swim to.

"Maybe I don't rate all your confidence. You know, I've never been sworn to testify in a malpractice case before. A good lawyer might sink me."

Swenson sounded surprised.

"You haven't? Well, no matter. It'll be as easy as pie. After all, aren't we the only ones who know what's really been going on and how silly the whole thing is? Right?"

"Oh sure."

"Look, I've really got to get back to my patients, but let me talk to you for just a second about an entirely different matter. I don't know if you're aware of it, but for some time now I've been running things out at the Municipal Hospital. The pay is rather good, and it takes hardly any of my time because there's always a third-year resident around, whom I can count on to handle most of it. But there are times when I do need to be away and other times when I'd just like someone to spell me. What I propose is that we share it together. So how would that suit you?"

This was an 'entirely different matter'? Who was kidding whom?

"I'm sure it'd be a privilege. When would I have to start?"

"Oh, no rush. No rush at all. Probably the best time would be right after the Stevens matter is disposed of. We wouldn't want to give anyone the wrong idea. Would we?"

"Of course not."

"Okay, Adam. Let's stay in touch."

"No problem."

None except that lying into thin air was one thing. There didn't seem to be much of a problem with that. It was part and parcel of everyday business. But doing it under oath would be unfamiliar territory and an experiment that could well turn sour. Worse, he couldn't think of any way to practice at it, to get it down real pat.

Adam decided to call up Irwin, a friend, and lawyer of his own, who handled tax matters for him. It was hard for Irwin to grasp his concerns. And well it should be, because Adam wasn't about to venture his inferentially accepted obligation to bend the truth under oath.

"Damned if I'm sure what you're asking me. Just go down there and tell the truth. That's all. You tell the truth and if they ask you for them, you turn over your office records. Then you're out of there and it's all over. What's so difficult about that?"

"It's not quite that simple."

"Since when? What's so complicated about the bald truth? In my experience, it's only the lies that get complicated. They take some heavy creativity."

"Look. Medicine is always a question of opinion and opinions aren't so simple."

"Who's gonna ask you your opinion about anything? Nobody, as far as I can see. You're not being called as an opinion expert for your beliefs as to what was done right or done wrong. You're being called solely as a treating physician, and as a witness to what is known as fact. So you just go in there and tell them what you did, and you're gone, dismissed. That's it."

"But..."

"There're no buts about it."

"Look, somewhere along the line, suppose quite innocently, it just simply happens that what I say doesn't come out quite the way I intended and..."

"So you say you're sorry, you correct yourself, and you move on. But truthfully, always truthfully. I hope I'm not hearing what I think I'm hearing. Those were pretty tricky words you were using."

"In a case like this, are there penalties for maybe volunteering a point of view not much different from that of the defendant?"

"Without believing it?"

"Well sort of."

"And without even being asked?"

"Well couldn't it happen once the questions started flying fast and furious, that it got, like blurted out?"

There was not a sound on the line. Adam took it as being, perhaps, a judicial pause. Then came Irwin's solemn sounding resumption.

"Why don't you just take your pick? There could be a simple reprimand, a couple of nights in jail, a perjury indictment. Be my guest. You wanta know something? I'm beginning to get your drift and I don't like it one bit. Or are you just looking for something to worry about? What the hell's going on, Adam?"

Adam decided on a different approach.

"After all, it's just a civil case. No? It's not like a criminal matter. Right?"

"Listen mister, you get up there and lie your fool head off to protect this guy, and pretty soon, you're gonna find out."

"Thanks Irwin. You've been a big help."

"My pleasure."

Twenty-six

By first indication, Zelma Stevens didn't appear to have hired herself much of a lawyer. He was rather young and arrived at Adam's office thirty minutes late, staying barely an hour. The deposition he conducted, consisted of no more than a single question, save for requesting the dates of Adam's examinations, and his physical findings.

"Now Doctor Merritt, is it a fair statement that you did, in point of fact, find cause for stopping the prednisone that had been prescribed for Mrs. Stevens by Doctor Swenson?"

"Yes. You might say so."

"Thank you sir. That's all I have."

So much apprehension and for what? It looked like he was home free. Free, if called to the witness stand by either side, to enlarge upon or qualify that limited statement howsoever he might choose. Or was he missing something? After all, he was new to this game. There might be a problem that for someone like himself, inexperienced in legal matters, was simply getting by him.

He decided, one night after dinner, to run the entire

matter past Annie, even confessing to his tacit understanding of an agreement to lend as much aid as possible to Swenson. Her reaction could have been anticipated.

"After all you've had to say about that dodo for years and years, you're gonna help him? I never heard of such a dumb thing."

"We've got to be practical once in awhile."

"Well save it for a different time and someone more deserving. If I've been hearing you right, that man's an absolute menace."

"Great, just great. I should cut my own throat by pulling the rug out from under him?"

"What would you stand to lose by telling the truth? A few bucks from Municipal Hospital? We can well afford to pass up on that one."

"Are you forgetting he's my chief, the full professor and chairman of my department?"

"So what? Maybe something good could come out of this mess. Isn't there a chance that if you go in there and level with everyone, tell it like it truly is, the school might get fed up and can that old buzzard? They could even put you in charge."

"It'd never happen. Testify against someone with Swenson's kind of clout and you're permanently out of the loop, dead in the water as far as academic advancement goes. Even worse things could happen."

"For instance?"

"I don't want to think about it. Doctors are a real nasty breed. They put out their own kind of contracts."

"And Mrs. Stevens? You don't care about what she's been put through?"

"Sure I do. But a few bucks aren't going to turn that

around. Either way, win or lose, she has no choice but to live with her deformity. It's not like a little money could reverse that and make her whole again."

"How about a lot of money, plus the satisfaction of righting a wrong? In your book, that doesn't count for anything?"

"What's she going to do with it? Buy a Rolls Royce or go live it up in Paris? And what's to be gained by being downright vindictive? We doctors are only human. No? We can make mistakes just like anyone else."

"So you should settle up and pay for them. And don't get cute with me about Rolls Royces or Paris. Maybe the money'd go for ways to make life a little easier for the poor woman. My God, you just finished telling me that she's dragging herself around in a walker."

"You quite finished? I don't even know why I brought it up."

"Why? I'll tell you why. Either you wanted someone to give the nod to what you yourself are having a hard time living with. Or you've become scared to death about not telling the truth, and need reassurance. That's why. Well you've come to the wrong person. I think that what you're planning to do is dead wrong, and if it all goes sour, you'll just have to take your lumps. So be it, and that's that. If you're looking for us, Willy and I are heading for the kitchen."

Annie called for the dog, got up from the dining room table, and took off. It wasn't that she'd actually stormed out, but she did leave a definite wake, in which Adam's thoughts were very much churning.

Adam was undeterred by his failed reach for support and his tumultuous turndown. But he felt he could well stand a drink, and not wanting to drink alone, he called his friend Harold, suggesting that he come over and share one.

Good old Harold, a retired chest surgeon and an amiable bear of a man, lived but a block away. Ever responsive to the prospect of agreable socializing, he was ringing the front doorbell in short order. Annie let him in. He was his usual cheery self.

"Hi there, kiddo. What's happening?"

"If you find a fire going in the den, it's only Adam doing one of his slow burns. You know what I mean? See if you can't go in there and douse it."

"Hey, that's a super line. How'd you come up with it?"

"I got inspired by him. Look. You know the way and right now, I'd like to steer clear of him."

"Boy, oh boy. What am I letting myself in for?"

Harold found Adam staring out a window and looking glum. The huge man promptly queried his host regarding the purpose of Adam's sudden invitation.

"Hey, dad. What's up? Annie's looking a little upset. And I thought that all you wanted was for us to get together and hoist a couple. You're not about to get me into some kind of a situation, are you? You know damned well that a dedicated bachelor like me is not in the least bit domestically oriented."

"When you going to stop calling me 'dad'? As far as I know, I've never had any kids. And you are at least six years older than me."

The nice thing about Harold was that he wasn't easily put off. Enviably good natured, he rolled relentlessly along.

"Now, now, let's not be picayune. It's just one of my favored figures of speech. That's all."

What with Adam acting the way he was, he didn't

take a chance on sitting down just yet. Rather, he took the liberty of heading straight for the liquor cabinet, but turned to Adam before invading it.

"What we got here? Anything new and interesting?"

Adam acted impatient with Harold's question, and even huffier than before.

"No. Same old stuff. Take whatever you want and give me my regular, please."

"What's your regular? Mine's single malt, straight up."

Adam continued to stare through the window.

"Same as the other time. The week before last."

"Hey, what is this? Some kind of a memory test? For Christ sake, Adam. What do you want to drink?"

"Vodka, any old kind, with one of those lemon twists and no ice."

Harold made the drinks, brought Adam's over to him, dropped into a facing armchair, and considering his cool reception, extended himself.

"Okay. I see something's been brewing. This isn't just about wanting a little company. So shoot. I'm all ears."

"And so much more."

Harold remained infinitely indulgent.

"Now, now. You know how hard it is for me to stick with any kinda diet. Particularly since I stopped doing surgery. Is that what we're gonna talk about? My waistline?"

Adam turned to his longtime friend. He'd broach the subject right off.

"You ever been sued?"

"Of course. Several times. Who hasn't?"

"Me, for one."

"That's amazing, really amazing. But then you don't ever get real sick patients. You know, life and death situations.

I used to think about being sued every time I opened someone's chest."

"So how did you handle it?"

Harold looked at him earnestly.

"Is that what this is all about? You're being sued?"

"No. Someone else. Doctor Swenson. Another dermatologist."

"The name doesn't ring a bell. Can't say I know him. What's his problem? He's got a lawyer. No?"

"Of course he has. That's not it. The question is how best to handle situations like this, when you're confronted with them. And I'm not exactly on the outside looking in. Both of us happen to have treated the same patient. The same patient who's now suing him. But they're gonna have questions for me as one of her treating doctors."

Harold, having by now downed half his glass, was leaning back in his chair, smiling at the ceiling, and starting to look a little beatific.

"Well I've no problem in telling you how I always handled it whenever I got sued. And mind you, I know damned well how most other guys dig in and make like Custer at that last stand of his. No matter what, they round up the wagons and tough it out to the bloody end. Maybe that's okay for them, but it's just not me."

"So?"

"Well, I sit myself down and go through all the medical records and the charges against me, looking to see if maybe there's really merit to the patient's claim. But let me tell you something! There've been times I knew damned well I'd done the wrong thing as soon as I'd done it."

"So then you called your insurance company?"

"Nope. The very first thing I'd do was to let the patient

and the family know there'd been a screw up, and that I was indeed very sorry."

"You out of your mind?"

"Why do you say that? Isn't that the really decent thing to do? Then, after that was taken care of, that's when I'd call the insurance company."

"Boy, I bet they just loved you for that."

"Well, according to the insurance policy, they're really supposed to get notified first. But I just knew they'd only ask me to clam up. And I could never stand to hear anything like that. If later on, they'd squawk about it, I'd simply say that all the concerned parties got the word within minutes of each other. So where'd be the beef? Know what I mean?"

"You're a shrewder devil than I ever gave you credit for."

"Hey old buddy, you've got it entirely wrong. This is not about being a devil. This is about not going to the devil."

Adam was given more than a little pause wih that one.

"Okay. What else?"

"Else? There is no else. When you're guilty, it's high time to insist that your insurance company pays up. If you don't believe you are, then you help them fight it. That's it. Simple as can be."

"You never stonewalled?"

"When I knew I was wrong?"

"Well you might not be sure of it."

"Hey, dad."

"What?"

"Sorry, sorry. I forgot. But there's no such thing. When you've blown it, you know it. You always know it. Anyone saying they don't is a damned liar."

Adam pressed him.

"So you never..."

"Lie about it? No sirree. It never pays to lie."

"Since when?"

"Look, I wasn't born yesterday. I'm just not prepared to pay that kinda price. That's all."

They both turned briefly meditative. Then Adam started up again.

"You get a lot of leads from your religion. No?"

"What's that? Some kinda leading question?"

"If it's too personal, I can understand. Even though I'm not a believer."

"You want a quick rundown on the origins and nature of guilt? Is that what you're after? And the tie-in with religion?"

Adam was in relentless pursuit of a good rationale for what could turn out to be sheer folly.

"So ultimately, the reason for being a standup guy, and on the level in cases like this, is so as not to feel guilty, should you do otherwise. Right?"

"You got a problem with that?"

"No, no problem. But no flair for it either."

Harold was looking up at the ceiling again.

"Gee dad, that's sad. Real sad."

"You addressing me or your celestial father?"

"Both, Adam. Both. And who you trying to kid? Because if what I suspect you're intending, wasn't already bugging the unholy hell out of you, you wouldn't be needing me to sit here for this dumb, roundabout kind of discussion. You'd be lifting one on your own."

Twenty-seven

Two months later, the case against Swenson was on the docket and Adam was subpoenaed to appear. Arriving at the courthouse well before his scheduled time, Adam took a seat at the rear to watch the goings on. He spotted Swenson sitting at an up front table, over on the right side, and near the judge's bench. Swenson was smiling broadly as two lawyers, whom Adam didn't recognize, appeared to be arguing something or other before the judge. Swenson continued to smile after they'd stopped and the judge had made an announcement.

"Defendant's motion to dismiss is denied."

Swenson's lawyer had not succeeded with his motion. The other lawyer, a well dressed, clean shaven fellow, acting as if he'd pretty much taken the judge's ruling for granted, stepped over to the remaining table and took a seat next to a humped over woman, easily recognizable as the unfortunate Mrs Stevens. This was someone obviously other than the young lawyer who'd conducted Adam's brief deposition.

As soon as the lawyers had retaken their seats, the judge called for everybody's attention.

"I think it's a little late to be starting our next witness. Why don't we break for lunch? Everyone be back here at two o'clock."

With that, the jurors--there were twelve of them, mostly men--got to their feet and filed out. Mrs Stevens' lawyer was bending over her and whispering something in her ear. With that, she turned and raised a hand, waving quite friendly like in Adam's direction. Meanwhile, Swenson was also gesturing and motioning him to come forward. Mrs. Stevens looked to be more than a little disappointed as Adam, rather than waving back at her, began to walk in the direction of Swenson's table.

Though he had no other choice, this opening move of his did not sit well with him. What he'd expected was to be called to the stand promptly upon his arrival in court, and at all costs not be made to look as if he were in league with anyone. Whatever he might be planning to declare in that courtroom, he didn't relish having it anticipated.

Before Swenson could say a word, Adam thumbed in the direction of Mrs Stevens' lawyer and raised the question that had been pressing him.

"Who's he?"

Swenson's own lawyer, a Currier Simpson, interceded.

"Oh, that's Mike Garvey. He's the senior partner in a big plaintiff's firm here in town. Don't let him fool you any. He'll come on real nice, but be looking for any way he can to just about skin you alive. They don't come more cagey."

"What's happened to that other fellow?"

"Who's that?"

"The one who took my deposition."

"Him? Oh he's what's called a leg man. One of the young lawyers used by their firm to take testimony before trial. They'd never trust anyone like that to actually try a case."

Swenson, wearing what looked to be a permanent smile, cut in to reassure him.

"Now don't you worry yourself over things like that, Adam. After all, you're only here to tell the simple truth and to set the record straight, once and for all. So why don't we all head across the street to Cavanagh's and have us a real nice lunch? How about it, my friend?"

"Well okay, I suppose."

Currier Simpson had words to add.

"That'll be quite all right. But remember now, we're not to discuss the case any. The judge has ruled that once testimony is under way, he wants no further discussions between the lawyers, the principals, or the experts. And besides that, you never know when you might be overheard by someone else, even a juror or two."

Adam, thinking he could well use a little legal direction, wasn't too happy about it.

"But I'm just one of the treating doctors. No?"

"It doesn't matter. Mum's the word. We're under instruction."

Cavanagh's was a crowded, noisy place, filled at the noon hour almost exclusively with lawyerly types. Just as well for there to be no discussion of the case. It would have required shouting to be heard, and those words would have been easily caught by anyone close by.

Menu in hand, the oddly pleased Swenson seemed set

on getting even more out of line, considering the grimness of the situation, as Adam viewed it.

"Well I'm going to have myself a lovely martini. Drinks, gentlemen?"

He had no takers. His own lawyer took exception to it.

"Why don't we skip the drinks? We've got to have our wits about us this afternoon. And let's not be taking anything for granted."

But Swenson was not to be denied.

"That's ridiculous. We are certain to prevail. Right, Adam? So we must drink to it."

By now Adam had many doubts and no comparable confidence.

"I'm going to skip the alcohol, also. Currier's right. There's no telling what's in store for us. And I particularly don't like the look of that lawyer she's hired. I have to tell you, he's got me worried."

Swenson was not to be dissuaded.

"Well, suit yourselves, gentlemen, and I'll do the same. Waiter, a martini, Bombay, well chilled, with an olive and straight up. So now, prime rib for everyone? Yes? So be it. One medium, two rare, and the roast potatoes. That should do it. We'll worry about our desserts a little later on."

Adam no more than sampled his prime rib and didn't touch the potatoes at all. It wasn't long for him, either, to become weary of listening to the irrelevant give and take between these two men, of golf, and rising college tuitions, and everything else they chose to gab about. His mind was entirely and expectantly focused on that marvelous moment when somehow having finished saying his obligatory piece, he'd be excused by the judge and permitted to head on home to Annie and Willy.

He was dead right to be worried about Mike Garvey. Right after lunch, Garvey called him to the witness stand. Hardly had Adam given his name and been sworn to tell the truth, but Garvey had a series of tough questions for him, to which had he given truthful answers, both he and Swenson would have been in the soup.

"Now Doctor Merritt, you're a friend of Doctor Swenson, are you not?"

"Not really. He's the chairman of my department, and as you know, a rather famous dermatologist with not only a national but a worldwide reputation."

Garvey blew his stack.

"Object! Move to strike! Your honor, would you please insist that the witness simply answer such questions with a yes or no and hold off from volunteering comments that aren't called for?"

The judge agreed.

"Sustained. Now Doctor Merritt, we'll all get done and be out of here a lot sooner if you just listen to the question very carefully and answer accordingly. The jury will disregard the last answer. Next question."

Garvey seemed needing to clear the air.

"Doctor Merritt. Are you or are you not a good friend of Doctor Swenson?"

In line with the judge's instruction, Adam not only listened carefully to the question, but also gave it full and rather extended consideration. However, he wasn't answering. He just sat there thinking about it. The court reporter and everyone else were staring at him expectantly.

Garvey was beside himself and the judge was pressed to find out what was going on.

"Doctor Merritt. Have you got a problem with that question?"

"Sure. I try to be friendly with just about everyone. And I'm really not sure what 'good' is supposed to mean. I simply don't want anyone to get the idea I'm some kind of a buddy to Doctor Swenson, because I'm not. And that would be getting it all wrong."

"Then why didn't you just say 'no' to Mister Garvey's question?"

"Well, all right, sir. My answer is no."

"Let's consider the question asked and answered, Mister Garvey. Next question."

Now Garvey was really mad. By subterfuge, Adam had gotten in some licks. And to Garvey's chagrin, a man he'd considered a straightforward fact witness, was turning out to be a hostile one.

"I object, your honor. I want that answer stricken also."

"Well it's not going to be. Motion denied and move on. Next question."

"Please note my exception to your honor's ruling."

"It's noted."

Garvey glowered at Adam. For awhile he looked like some maddened bull, ready to paw the ground and charge. But then he took a different, a softly worded tack, and led Adam through the various details of his diagnosis, examination, and treatment of Mrs. Stevens. He spent the better part of an hour at it. Every time Adam chanced to look over at Swenson, the man was sporting that same indulgent smile. And every time he happened to look at Mrs. Stevens, she had a worried look about her. Then finally, Garvey and he were set to face off over the nitty gritty of this whole unpleasant business.

"Doctor Merritt. Do you remember the very last answer you gave at the time of your deposition in this matter?"

"Yes."

"Have you reread it recently?"

"Yes I have."

"Well I'm going to hand it to you now, and I ask you to just read it over to yourself. Okay.?"

"Sure."

As soon as Adam had done as requested, Garvey, looking not at him but straight at the jurors, posed what he obviously thought to be the critical follow up question.

"Do you still hold with what you said there, Doctor Merritt?"

"Yes."

"All right, sir. Now would you please read that question aloud as well as your answer, just as you gave it back then, for the benefit of the jury?"

Adam read from the transcript of his previous deposition.

"'Question: Now, Doctor Merritt, is it a fair statement that you did, in point of fact, find cause for stopping the prednisone that had been prescribed for Mrs. Stevens by Doctor Swenson? Answer: Yes. You might say so.'"

Garvey, hell bent on just about nailing Adam's words to the wall, gave vent to his satisfaction.

"There. That wasn't so difficult, was it, doctor? Your honor, I'm through with this witness."

It was then that Adam, assuming he also had the privilege of some kind of a final say, popped off with his own last words on the subject at hand.

"Right. You might say so. And you might say a lot of other things also. Because it's impossible for anyone to say exactly what brought on the collapse of Mrs. Stevens' spine. Stopping the prednisone was a purely precautionary move on my part."

Garvey went ballistic. His Irish was up and boiling over.

"I object, your honor. This is an out and out disgrace. There was no question pending for this witness. What he said was entirely gratuitous and completely out of line. I demand that you admonish him and ask the jury to ignore his little speech."

Then Currier Simpson stood up with his own indignant retort.

"To the contrary, your honor. Mister Garvey did in fact pose a question to the witness. He asked him if it, and I quote, wasn't so difficult for him to have given his prior response. And Doctor Merritt, responding in a perfectly appropriate and logical manner, told him, and I quote him again right, to indicate that in truth it hadn't been at all difficult, and then he gave the reasons for it not being so. There was a question, an answer, and a completely appropriate explanation of the answer."

The judge stared down at the two lawyers, and for a few seconds said nothing. Then he turned towards Adam.

"Doctor. Don't get the idea I don't know what you're up to. I do and I don't like it. I don't like it one little bit."

Adam's hands grew cold and his head was shaking side to side. Would he be heading for a big fine, or worse, a night in jail?

But then the judge turned to Garvey.

"On the other hand Mister Garvey, I have to admit there's something to what Mister Simpson is saying. Why didn't you just leave well enough alone? Why'd you have to celebrate with that 'that wasn't so difficult, is it?' business.

If that couldn't be taken as a final question to the witness, then I've got to admit I don't know what would. Just because the doctor was sharp enough to see an opening and get in a few licks, doesn't mean we've got to bail you out for asking a real dumb and redundant question. And as for him going on too long and explaining his answer, I'm going to allow it. A witness is still entitled to give full answers and explanations as long as I'm presiding. So objection overruled."

Then the judge addressed Simpson.

"Mister Garvey's said he's through with this witness. Any questions for Doctor Merritt, Mr. Simpson?"

"I've none at all, your honor."

"Then the witness is excused."

Adam was numb. But not so numb he didn't appreciate that by having no questions for him, Simpson had precluded any possibility of a redirect examination of him by Garvey, by which he could possibly do his testimony considerable damage.

As he left the courtroom, Adam sort of sensed that Swenson, who was still beaming, could very well want to hug him.

Twenty-eight

O ver the next two weeks, Swenson would phone from time to time, keeping Adam up to date on how things were going down at the courthouse. He was pleased to report that Mrs. Stevens case against him had been crippled in several ways. Adam's testimony had taken her lawyer entirely by surprise. And having had the usual difficulty recruiting good medical experts, so commonly the case for plaintiff lawyers, Garvey had expected Adam's testimony would sway the jury. That had proved to be a major tactical error.

For his part, Swenson had no difficulty at all in corralling experts to testify in his behalf. One by one they'd been filing into the courtroom and re-trumpeting what Adam had put in place, as a kind of party line, for them to follow. To whit, that what had happened to Mrs. Stevens was a matter of speculation, the prednisone being of unproved significance.

Swenson even got an endocrinologist to recite a dozen or more reasons older women might get osteoporosis. And the jury, made up exclusively of men, could hardly be expected to find the subject of what happens to post menopausal women, the least bit interesting. So for the most part, they let much of what was being said, go right by them.

Swenson's final phone call was to sound his triumph. There had been a defendant's verdict.

"Just like I was telling you from the very beginning, Adam. It was in the bag. That's not to say you weren't very, very helpful. As a matter of fact, in my humble opinion, you are what I call a winner, an up and coming winner. By the way, as soon as I put together that new schedule of ours for Municipal Hospital, you know, the one we talked about, I'll be getting it in the mail to you. Thanks again, my friend."

Adam couldn't bring himself to let on right away, as to what had been the outcome of the trial. Annie had to get it from the next day's morning paper. After she'd read it through, all she had, was a couple of questions.

"Boy oh boy, I wonder how poor Mrs. Stevens took that stupid verdict. Tough, huh? Well, are you happy now?"

"Who's ever supposed to be happy? Not me, certainly."

"Oh, by the way, you know that old radio of yours?"

"Of course."

"Well I finally got the hang of turning it on and off. Actually, right after you left this morning I was using it to pick up WRH, and for a change, it wasn't sounding half bad. But then, while I'm in the next room, doing my ironing, all of a sudden the music stops and I smell something burning. So I rushed back inside and yanked the plug from the wall. If I hadn't been right next door, and doing my ironing, the whole house could have burned down. Damned if that thing was not on fire, Adam--the cabinet was even starting to melt! I had to douse it with some water, and even the electric wall socket was scorched black. I know how much that old radio means to you, my dear, being a reminder of your Bellevue days. But I rather doubt there's gonna be any saving it now. And just as well, it could have done us in!"